MW00931868

# TALES FROM FINNEGAN'S WAKE

*An Assortment of Suspenseful, Fantastical,
Tragic, Romantic, Humorous, and Provocative
Stories Originally Published by Literary Journals
and Zines in the US and Overseas*

## By Bill Finnegan

## Illustrations and Cover Art by Raven OKeefe

ISBN: 1492189588
ISBN-13: 978-1492189589

Library of Congress Control Number: 2013915534
CreateSpace Independent Publishing Platform
North Charleston, South Carolina

*For my family.*

# CONTENTS

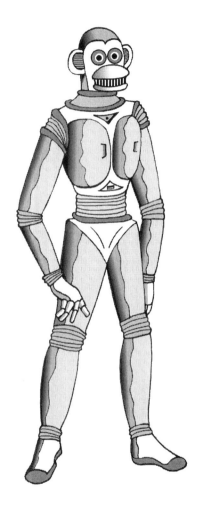

"Although the interview left Charles satisfied
with Bob's qualifications, he found Bob's
appearance to be rather off-putting."

# PROGRAMMING IS EVERYTHING

Within the darkened opera house, the second Act of *Madam Butterfly* was drawing to a close. Cho-Cho-San and her little boy knelt inside her small hilltop house looking down at the harbor where Lieutenant Pinkerton's ship was moored. He had been gone for three years, and Cho-Cho-San had almost given up hope he would return and see the son she had borne him. A DramaScent system surrounded the audience with the aroma of the sea and of the celebratory flowers adorning the little bamboo house. From the ceiling and four corners of the opera house, courtesy of its innovative Acoustiwrap design, came the unprocessed sound of a chorus of sopranos and tenors humming a tender melody that gave no hint of the tragedy that was to follow.

As he sat in the audience, Charles was aware something was bothering him but could not put his finger on it. The tickets had been expensive, so the distraction was very irritating. He quickly went over the events of the day hoping to pinpoint the source of his concern.

———

At breakfast he and his wife noticed that their nannydroid, Monique, had developed a stutter. Fearing this foreshadowed a systems crash, Charles took Monique to the maintenance department of the dealership where he purchased her.

"She's going to be babysitting for our three-year-old twin boys tonight, so I need to be sure she's okay," he told the technician behind the counter.

"I've started stuttering," Monique added helpfully, "and we wa-want to be su-sure my CPU won't lock up."

"I'm afraid we can't look at her today, but you can leave her and we'll let you have Bob, a loaner, who'd be a perfect babysitter," the technician said. "Used to take care of the dogs and cats waiting for adoption at the Hinesville animal shelter before it closed. A local nursery school has used him dozens of times, and they say he really loves small kids. Very gentle and protective, and he charms them with cute stories about the animals he cared for. He's only five years old, has a seventy-two-hour battery, and an impressive one-forty AIQ, so he's a lot smarter than Monique. Was a jack-of-all-trades at the shelter. Closed it down almost singlehandedly.

If after trying him you like him enough to buy him, we'd let you have him for twenty percent below blue book with a good trade-in price for Monique."

Charles knew manufacturers were notorious for inflating artificial intelligence quotas, and dealerships routinely hinted their droids possessed that holy grail of artificial intelligence research, empathy. This was potentially dangerous because it gave buyers a false sense of security. As it was, the latest household droids had such pleasant voices and attractive virtual personalities it was easy to forget they had no compassion and morality to fall back on in situations not anticipated by software designers. However, they all were programmed to reject commands that used so-called "words of harm," and this had proved effective. Charles's only concern was whether Bob, who was designed to work with animals, knew enough about caring for children. So he painstakingly questioned the droid about this for half an hour, giving special attention to how he would react in various emergency scenarios.

"What would you do, Bob, if one of the boys got food stuck in his windpipe?"

"I have been programmed to deal with that, Sir. At the shelter, I would watch the children for signs of distress when they ate the candy I gave them. If the child can make sounds and cough loudly, I know the airway blockage is mild and can let him or her cough up the food. Otherwise I need to act quickly and perform the Heimlich maneuver on children over one year of age or administer back slaps and two-finger chest thrusts to infants. Of course, the amount of force I use has to be commensurate with the child's size."

Although the interview left Charles satisfied with Bob's qualifications, he found Bob's appearance to be rather off-putting. Like Monique, he was a chrome-plated semi-android. But while Monique's face, limbs, and movements were somewhat human-like, Bob had very long arms, moved about like a giant chimpanzee, and had his sensory nodes and speaker grill configured to give him a grinning chimp-like affair for a face. Charles wondered whether Bob's designers had selected the chimp motif to charm children visiting the animal shelter. Primatologists would consider the choice ironic because chimpanzees in the wild were a violent species in which males commonly killed infants so the mothers would mate. But Charles knew that his boys, who were very fond of stories about Curious George the monkey, would love Bob at first sight, and really that was all that mattered.

⸻

On stage the touching vigil of mother and child continued. Subtle changes in lighting and music signaled the passage of time. The moon was now up, and Cho-Cho-San's little boy suddenly slumped against her as he fell asleep. At that moment Charles recalled overhearing a conversation between his wife and Bob shortly before they left for the opera.

"The boys are a challenge at bed time. They'll want you to play games and read them one book after another, and that's okay, but I want you to put them to sleep by eight o'clock no matter what."

"Put them to sleep?" Bob asked, sounding bewildered.

"That's right. Haven't you done that before?"

"Yes, but with children it has just been naps."

"They napped this afternoon. Tonight you put them to sleep."

Bob thought about this for a few seconds. "Any particular way?"

His wife laughed. "Any way that works."

Charles moaned and bolted from his seat just as the curtain began to descend on Act II. The rest of the audience remained in place to applaud, so there was no one to obstruct his dash up the center aisle. He burst through the double doors into the brightly lit lobby, pulled out his Omnicom, and shouted "home." Bob's grinning face appeared on the screen.

"Oh good, it is you, Sir. I am sorry to say there was a complication here, but I think I handled it properly. The boys and I began a game of hide-and-seek at 7:49. Your house is very large and, unfortunately, it took me until 8:04 to find them. This made it impossible to carry out your wife's exact instructions, which were to put them to sleep by eight o'clock. So I was faced with the issue of whether she would still want me to do it. After carefully weighing the—"

"For God's sake, what'd you do?"

"Why, I let them take naps."

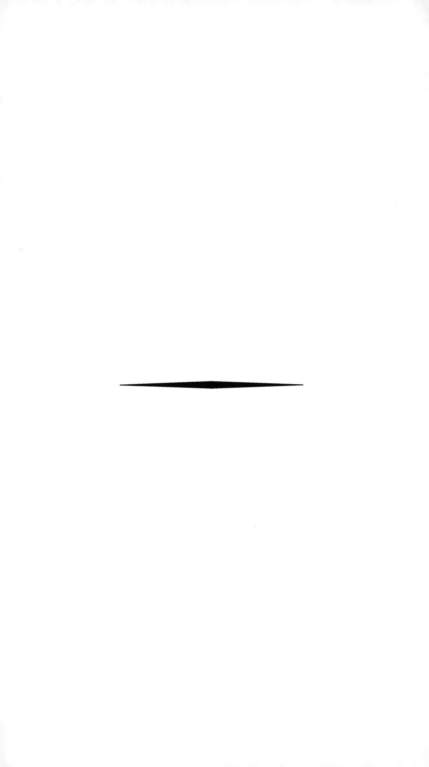

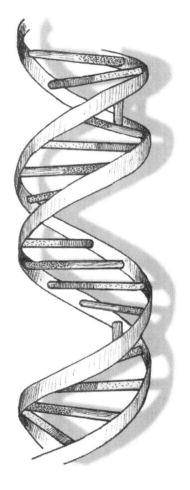

*"Suppose the passenger represents
a genetic mutation?"*

# ALPHA TEST

Paul Redford had wanted to visit a desert ever since seeing the movie "Lawrence of Arabia" many years previous. So he was glad to finally be in one, even though the part of the Mojave he was traveling through was splattered with small vegetation that gave it the equivalent of a five o'clock shadow.

Redford had rented a car in Las Vegas and was on his way to a meeting at New Charon Research Corp. Their Public Relations Director, Anna Flores, had called him the prior afternoon at his office in New Jersey and offered him $500 an hour plus expenses to drop everything and fly to Nevada.

A Google search of "New Charon Research" produced nothing he didn't already know: it was seeking to extend the human lifespan through physics; it had a 20-mile long particle accelerator, the Moorlock Disperser-Compressor, buried under the Mojave; and it was owned by Toby Moorlock, a multibillionaire global telecommunications mogul who was notorious for his cutthroat business practices and anachronistic espousal of social Darwinism.

It took Redford two hours of driving on secondary roads to reach the New Charon campus, which consisted of a high chain link fence enclosing a vast expanse of desert and two structures—a small booth at the entrance gate and a large building a mile away. The guard at the gate told him to make a U-turn and park in the small visitor's lot where Ms. Flores would pick him up.

Ten minutes later, a tan expedition-type Range Rover with Anna Flores at the wheel drove into the lot and pulled alongside his rental.

"Hi, Doctor Redford, I'm Anna," she said with a sunny smile. "May I call you Paul?"

"Sure. I'm happy to meet you, Anna."

Still single at thirty-eight, Redford processed that she was pretty, about his age, and wasn't wearing a ring on her left hand. The combination of the vehicle and her outfit—a khaki blouse and slacks—made it look like she was on Safari. Redford felt overdressed in the black suit, white shirt, and dark tie he always wore when acting in a professional capacity.

As soon as he climbed into the Rover, she handed him a non-disclosure agreement and waited until he read and signed it before driving away.

While she drove, she explained that her boss, New Charon's president, Bob King, told her to find an expert on religion who wasn't a fanatical nut job. Redford was a practicing psychologist with a doctorate in theology whose specialty was religion-related mental illness. Flores chose him on the basis of his performance in a televised criminal trial at which he had testified as an expert for the defense. Privately she was glad he looked as distinguished in person as he had on television.

"Bob wants an expert on religion who can be objective about it. I hope that's you."

"Let me put it this way. What's important to me religion-wise is finding what I can reasonably believe in, or at least hope for, regarding God and my ultimate fate, which requires a lot of thought and study. I'm so continually testing and wrestling with my conclusions that I've come to feel as much of an affinity to atheists as to true believers, although not with the smug, aggressive version of either. There's way too much that's profoundly mysterious in the Universe to allow for complacency. Einstein, an agnostic, wrote an essay titled 'Strange Is Our Situation Here on Earth' in which he waxed poetic about how a sense of the mystical is the most beautiful emotion we can experience. He said that at the center of all true religiousness, science, and art is 'the knowledge that what is impenetrable to us really exits, manifesting itself as the highest wisdom and the most radiant beauty, which our dull faculties can comprehend only in their most primitive forms.' I love that so much I have it tacked to my bulletin board."

"Good. That's about where I am. Now we have only ten minutes, so I'm going to talk fast and keep it simple. Physicists have long known that the particles that make up the reflected light and sound waves that enable us to see and hear, and the electrical waves emitted by the synapses in our brains, all drift off into space. All this information from the past was thought to remain in the universe, but was considered to be too distant for retrieval. New Charon scientists have discovered that when these particles, consisting at the upper level of electrons and protons, leave earth's gravitational field they merge and morph into a stream of what they call 'Stark-Neutrino Hybrid particles.' The stream combines with other similar streams to form a river of chronological data, which, instead of heading off into the outer reaches of the Universe, circles round the earth. We call this river the 'Reel' because we think of it as a three-dimensional movie film that is continuously playing our past."

"Can you retrieve data from it?"

"Better than that. Our scientific team under Harold Stark has developed a process of particle modification that enables us to insert humans, 'quantum-nauts' or 'Q-nauts' we call them, into the Reel and bring them back by converting them from electrons and protons to Stark-Neutrinos and then back again. And we're able to locate specific dates on the Reel through a technique that's analogous to carbon dating."

"Time travel!"

"No, we aren't visiting the past, only a record of it. So if we disrupt things nothing is affected in our time."

"But I thought you're looking for ways to expand life expectancy."

She flashed a proud little smile. "We hope to soon have the capability to go into the Reel and bring a person back after his or her death at whatever age he or she specified in advance. 'Return to Life' or 'RTL' is our tentative name for the service, which will be affordable only by the very wealthy."

"But what you bring back won't be real, it'll only be a simulacrum."

"Call it what you like. The important thing is it'll be identical to the original in all respects, including its memories."

Redford doubted this was possible but knew he had to suspend his skepticism if he wanted to earn a fee. "Well now I can understand why you hired me. Offering a secular way to achieve what is arguably a kind of eternal life could have a disruptive effect on organized religion. It might trigger a turf war."

"And we'll need your help in managing that."

"I'll do my best, but it's a can of worms. Populist politicians may also be problem, considering RTL will benefit only the wealthy upper class."

She smiled. "Oh, but that's not the case! Toby will also be using it pro bono to retrieve eminent individuals whose return would benefit all of humankind. It's what I like most about RTL."

"That could help or hurt a lot, depending on whom he chooses," Redford said grimly as he recalled reports of Moorlock subsidizing a flattering biography of Joseph Stalin and praising Hitler's charisma.

She pulled into a parking space in front of a low, windowless building with four enormous dish antennas on its roof.

"This is headquarters. It's built on the same theory as the desert Indian pit houses—ten percent above ground, ninety percent below. Both our business offices and the operations center for the accelerator are here."

———

The meeting took place in a beige windowless room containing a circular conference table. Dazzling Navajo rugs were spread around the floor, and ornately framed photos of Toby Moorlock hung on three walls like Byzantine icons. Redford thought votary candles would not be out of place. On the fourth wall there was a large flat screen monitor wirelessly connected to a player on the table.

Bob King, New Charon's president, greeted Redford and introduced him to Asher Barr, general counsel, Harold Stark, head of research, and Jack Bold, the owner of Bold Security, an outside contractor. All were in their late forties or early fifties, impeccably groomed, and dressed in business casual attire—long-sleeved, collared shirts and creased trousers—with the addition of a white lab coat in Stark's case and a black eye patch in Bold's.

King, who was in high spirits, asked Bold to bring Flores, Barr, and Redford up-to-speed on an unexpected development. Bold rose and walked to the wall-mounted monitor.

"The Q-naut I assigned to Alpha Test 5 is Dave Santini, a thirty-year-old ex-Navy Seal. Up till now the Alphas have been quick in-and-out affairs. But this time the Q-naut was to travel around and find a specific individual, engage him in conversation, and return alone by activating a new Max-2 launcher-converter. It was a test of the Max-2 and a dry run for the Beta Test during which the Q-naut will find a deceased individual, probably Mr. Moorlock's mother, and bring her back. Alpha 5 would have been a piece of cake but for the point of entry, which I understand, was selected as a kind of lark by Mr. Moorlock."

Bold used a remote to start the disc player. A steel booth with a glass front appeared on the monitor. It contained two barely discernable human figures who appeared to be caught in a blizzard. The picture cleared, and the men came into sharp focus. Both were lean, bearded, and dressed in long-sleeved Arab-style tunics. One stood slightly stooped as though he were injured. The other had the remnant of a monk's bag slunk over his shoulder. It looked like it had been blown apart by something it contained. The booth opened and the man with the bag remnant stepped out and spoke: "I'm sorry, everyone, but I just couldn't let them crucify him."

Barr gasped, "Jesus Christ."

"Exactly," King said, and everyone laughed, except Redford and Flores.

"Of course, that will be the last time we send one of Bold Security's muscle heads on a mission," Stark said.

Bold turned red. "You don't know what you're talking about. Santini has a one hundred thirty IQ, and it took him only three months to learn Aramaic from Iraqi goat herders. Problem is that his specialty in the Seals was hostage rescue, and in the heat of the moment he reverted to it."

"Where is the Passenger now?" Flores asked Bold.

"He's resting in the infirmary. We treated him for head and back wounds and dehydration, and he's fine. He's remarkably composed and talks a lot with Santini, the only one here who speaks Aramaic. But we don't know what he's saying because Santini is being extremely protective and not very forthcoming. He'll only say that the Passenger has lots of questions."

"He's bonded with him. It was a mistake to assign a Christian to this Mission," Stark said angrily.

Bold howled with delight, apologized for the outburst, and announced, slowly and softly, that Santini was a Jew.

"Let's get back to business," King said. "Toby is due here in three hours so we don't have much time to put together an action plan. The situation in a nutshell is that Santini's impulsiveness has turned an alpha test into a successful beta. So we are now able to announce the RTL capability in context of a spectacular extraction. I also see an opportunity for Toby to build a profit center around the Passenger who is about to become the world's number one celebrity. I'm thinking of books, speaking engagements, inspirational CDs and DVDs, product endorsements. Asher, I want you to draft an employment contract as soon as we finish here."

"Sure. In English and Aramaic. Santini can help."

"Santini only speaks Aramaic," Bold said. "The guys he learned it from couldn't read or write."

"Find someone who can," King said. "Maybe Dr. Redford can help." He turned to Flores. "I want a plan for operationalizing all of this on my desk within the hour."

"Right," she said. "I expect Toby will want to introduce the Passenger to the world on television. They would each make a statement and then answer questions from a panel of prominent journalists, academicians, and religious leaders."

She paused to allow King to comment and then continued.

"I assume Toby would report the successful beta test, describe the technology, and announce RTL. I'm open to ideas on what the Passenger, who will be speaking through an interpreter, might want to say. I suppose he would refer to his biblical message, the main points of which were…"

"Get ready for the Kingdom of God," Barr offered jovially.

Redford was happy for the opportunity to contribute. "There are also his ethical teachings and his characterization of God as a loving father, which was new and not part of Jewish tradition or, as far as I know, of any other religious tradition."

"A Tsunami kills 200,000 Indonesians. I call that extremely tough love," Stark said.

"Read the Book of Job," Redford snapped, wishing he could have thought of something better.

King shook his head. "No, all that's old news. Everyone has heard it already. He needs a new message. Something meaningful and exciting to people today. Toby will want to draft it himself."

"The Passenger's wardrobe will require some thought," Flores said.

Barr chuckled. "Yeah, the tunic and beard make him look like a terrorist."

King thought about it. "Maybe something a new age shaman would wear or the Maharishi yogi. Or even a business suit. Anna, have the art department do sketches of him in different kinds of outfits for Toby to consider."

Redford was amazed by their obliviousness to the wonder and the mind-boggling potential of the situation.

"With all due respect, I think you're overlooking a couple of things," he said, determined for Flores's sake not to sound like a fanatical nut job.

Everyone turned to him.

"You're assuming he'll do what you tell him and, even more important, you seem to be forgetting that he, or the original version of him, is sacred to over two billion Christians worldwide."

King stared at him blankly. "Your point?"

"That you're about to walk into a minefield. If the public believes the Passenger is who you say he is and you disrespect him, there'll be riots. There'll also be riots if they consider him a fraud or, even worse, the antichrist. He probably won't match their preconceptions of him and his second coming."

"We could apologize for perceived disrespect," Flores said gravely, "but it would be a disaster if the public thinks the Passenger is a fraud. It would ruin the market for RTL."

"That's right," Barr said, "and the Christian churches might lobby for a law prohibiting RTL as a form of human cloning."

King was unfazed. "I'm sure our fellow Christians will prove to be more adaptable than you think. The Tibetan Buddhists have no problem with having the Dali Lama, a laid back regular guy, as a kind of demigod."

Redford figured King did not like being con-
tradicted, and he proceeded gingerly. "You're right
about the Tibetans, Sir. That's part of their ancient
tradition and is supported by their religious leaders. But my best guess is that the Christian clergy
will be skeptical and maybe even worried about the
Passenger's identity, and that the Vatican will con-
vene an investigatory proceeding like the ones they
use to vet potential saints. It could go on for years."

Stark was still bristling from the Book of Job re-
tort and wanted another round. "It takes them so
long because they need to find miracles they can attribute to the candidate. But our man can perform
them at will, isn't that so Doctor Redford?"

"I'm not convinced you really have him, or
all of him, in the infirmary. As I understand it, the
Passenger is comprised of a pattern of particles that
you have converted from a different pattern of different kinds of particles. There must be some possibility of error, of things falling between the cracks."

"The algorithms give us back our Q-nauts exactly as they were before, and the same is true of the
Passenger," Stark insisted.

"Suppose the Passenger represents a genetic
mutation, an anomaly with particles that differ from
the norm in some way. Say an evolutionary process
that God—or a blind primal force, if you prefer—set
in motion produced a human with special psychic or
intellectual capabilities that connect him in a unique

way to the Deity or the Cosmos. Can you be sure your algorithms would be up to handling that?"

"No, I can't, because your supposition is too vague, besides being reminiscent of the Nestorian heresy and therefore outside the pale of Christian orthodoxy. Let's suppose, on the other hand, that he was in fact processed correctly and completely. Is it your position that he would be able to perform miracles?

"Well, the most significant ones, the post-crucifixion appearances, can't be replicated because he was rescued."

"Suppose he gives a speech and some screwball takes him out with an assault rifle. Would that be good enough?" Barr asked with a grin.

Stark chuckled. "And what about walking on water?"

Flores, who knew Redford was dodging the question for her sake, came to his rescue. "It doesn't matter. New Testament-type miracles won't be enough to impress a public that's been jaded by movie special effects, high-tech stage magicians, and faith-healing televangelists. Let's move on. We're wasting time."

Stark removed a vibrating smart phone from his pocket, read a text message, and left.

"I don't mean to pile on Bob," Barr said, "but since we are looking at risk factors I need to point out that the Passenger is an undocumented Palestinian alien, and we are right this minute violating immi-gration law by harboring him."

"Don't quit on me, people," King pleaded. "Profit motive aside, don't you think we have an obligation to introduce this fascinating man to the world?"

"Shouldn't we let him decide that?" Redford asked.

Barr agreed. "If we hold him against his will, he can sue us for damages in civil court on grounds of what's called 'false imprisonment.' You know how litigious Jews are. He could recover millions, and it would be no consolation to Toby if he gave it all to the poor."

"Wouldn't it make sense to help him stay out of the limelight until he's been taught English and mod-ern history and gradually exposed to our society?" Flores asked.

"He could stay with me," Redford said eagerly. "That would protect you from immigration law problems."

Flores saw that King was floundering and threw him a life preserver. "But this is really Toby's call."

"Right," he said, "and I need a PowerPoint pre-sentation that tees-up the pros and cons of going public and that outlines a public relations and mar-keting plan in case Toby chooses that option. You have an hour. Asher and Dr. Redford will help."

Stark returned.

"Problems solved," he said to King with mock cheerfulness. "He's gone."

"What?"

"He's broken up and presumably drifted back to the Reel."

"How could this happen?"

"Remember, Santini was converted from electrons and protons to Stark-Neutrinos and then back again. The Passenger was a one-way conversion that, for some reason, hasn't held."

"Damn, this is terrible. Toby will be furious."

"May I speak with Santini?" Redford asked Bold, who nodded his consent.

"Me too," Flores said, and the three of them left the room.

"How much of a setback is this?" King asked.

"I don't know. It may have happened because he was going to die soon after we extracted him. Or maybe we reached back too far on the Reel. Our next probe should be into a much more recent date, say one in the 1950s. The Stark-Neutrinos may be more susceptible to permanent conversion. And we should pick a passenger with at least twenty years of life left on the Reel. But you're right about Toby. Someone's head will have to roll, and we have to make sure it's not one of ours. First thing when you talk to him say Bold screwed up by supplying a mentally unbalanced Q-naut. I'll beat the same drum when he gets here."

"Good, I'll call him now. You get ready to convince him you have a good handle on what went wrong and can fix it. It'll help if you focus his attention on the details of the next mission, which has to include an extraction."

"Yeah, but I don't want it to be Toby's mother until we're sure we've got it right."

"How about Elvis?" Barr asked.

*"Confucius knew the question was important."*

# RECIPROCITY

Harry Markus and his wife, Ellen, had returned home from a Western Caribbean cruise the previous night. They slept late and, after breakfast, unpacked their belongings and found places for the two souvenirs they had bought. One was a painting of fishing boats being pulled onto a beach by natives. Ellen thought it stunning, Harry, kitschy. They hung it over their living room sofa. The other souvenir was a statuette in the Aztec or Mayan style of a stubby man who was angrily pressing his fists together and displaying a mouth full of pointed teeth. Ellen hated it as much as Harry loved it, but agreed to display it on a shelf in their house's entrance foyer.

Later that day, as he was paying bills in his home office, Harry heard a chain saw start up. He knew immediately what was going on. His new neighbor, Rick, whom he and Ellen privately referred to as the "redneck from hell," had begun cutting down trees to make room in his backyard for an asphalt parking area. It was for an assortment of the 1960s-era cars Rick favored because their lack of electronics allowed him to repair and maintain them himself. He needed at least six of them, he joked, to be sure at least one would be in working condition.

But in all other ways, Rick was a good neighbor. He never saw Harry working in the yard without lending a hand or providing a tool that made the job easier. And he had promised that come winter he would clear snow from Harry's sidewalk and driveway with his state-of-the art snow blower. So Harry and Ellen were, in a sense, obliged to tolerate the backyard parking lot.

Harry went downstairs to view the devastation from his kitchen window. Ellen was already there.

"There goes the view from our back porch," she said. "It's going to be ugly as hell. It'll take at least fifty thousand off the value of our house."

Harry sensed he would soon have a migraine if he didn't relax. "Look, honey, we've decided not to complain to the zoning board, so let's try to focus on the good things Rick does for us." He took an aspirin and returned to his home office.

He was doing his best to ignore the chain saw and finish his paperwork when he heard a loud crash and a scream from Rick's yard. He ran down the stairs and out the back door to the fence. Rick was lying on his back with a large oak tree across his grotesquely flattened chest. His eyes were wide open in surprise and blood was gushing from his mouth.

"Resuscitate him, resuscitate him," Ellen half shouted, half screamed.

"It won't help. Look at his chest," Harry said and then vomited.

The funeral was held three days later. Rick had a wife and four young children, so it could not have been sadder. Harry left for work right after the church ceremony, leaving Ellen to represent them at the burial. She was going to tell Rick's wife that she would be available to babysit and help in any other way she could, and that Harry, who was a lawyer, would be happy to answer any legal questions she might have.

When Harry arrived at his office, his secretary, who looked worried, handed him a phone message saying that Howard Partridge, one of the law firm's senior partners, wanted to see him as soon as he got in.

Partridge's secretary ushered Harry into a large office. The walls were covered with prints and paintings of men shooting lions, elephants, and other big game, as though to emphasize that, despite his game bird surname, Partridge was to be counted among the hunters, not the hunted.

"Sit down Markus," he said with unusual warmth.

"Thank you, sir."

"Care for some coffee or tea? I hear you've had a rough morning."

"No thanks."

Partridge stared at him noncommittally for a few seconds before continuing.

"Do you know Confucius was once asked if there was a single word that explained how society functioned?"

"No, I've never heard that."

"Well, old Confucius knew the question was important and that his reputation was at stake, so he thought about it for a long while, carefully considering all the possibilities. Guess what he finally came up with?"

"I have no idea."

"'Reciprocity!' The answer he gave was 'reciprocity,' a brilliant insight that is supported by modern science. Studies of primates, including us humans, strongly suggest reciprocity is part of our DNA, which means we are, in effect, programmed to do unto others as they do unto us. And indeed you see reciprocity in play all around us, even here at our law firm. Lawyers who are conscientious and produce good results are handsomely rewarded. Those who don't…well, you know."

Partridge paused and stared at Harry, who nodded to signal he got the drift.

"I needed your help this morning, Markus. Goodyear's CEO called at nine. Said she was preparing for a tough board meeting and needed to know the status of the settlement negotiations in the Freegate litigation. To my chagrin I couldn't provide it because our lead counsel on the case is taking a short, well earned vacation, and his second-in-command, namely you, was at a funeral with his cell phone turned off—a neighbor's funeral, according to your secretary. Of course paying your respects was a good thing, a necessary thing. But you could have done it by sending flowers and a card, and been here on time."

"There was nothing on my schedule, and I'm only an hour late," Harry said in a pleading tone.

Partridge sneered at the excuse. "We're going to be doing some downsizing next month, and I'm thinking you'd probably do better someplace else where you felt more of a sense of urgency about your work."

As he drove home that evening, Harry rehearsed what he would tell Ellen. He knew his career at the firm was over, even though Partridge's words left room for a change of heart. The man had always disliked him, so this incident would finish him for sure. Finding a job at his age in the current market was going to be difficult.

Following a sleepless night, Harry returned to work the next morning to find the firm's business at a standstill. The entire staff was standing around in small groups talking softly.

His secretary spotted him and left a cluster of gossipers. "Read this," she said, indicating an article in the newspaper she handed him. It reported that at approximately seven thirty the previous evening, a tractor trailer traveling north on the Turnpike had crossed the divider and collided head-on with a southbound Corvette driven by one Harold Partridge. A photo showed the Corvette crushed flat as a pancake.

"I hope Mrs. Partridge didn't have to identify the body," his secretary remarked grimly.

Harry returned the paper without commenting, went into his office, and closed the door.

He had been elated by the news and was disgusted with himself. True he had a good reason to hate Partridge, and his life would be better with him gone. But the man had died horribly and it was monstrous of him to be pleased about it, even if everyone was born with a reciprocity gene as Partridge claimed.

Even worse, Harry feared that his ill will, first toward his neighbor and then toward his boss, had somehow caused their deaths. But on reflection that did not make sense. To conclude that the hostile feelings had caused the accidents simply because they preceded the accidents was a textbook example of the "*post hoc ergo propter hoc*" logical fallacy. And the real explanation was obvious. Cutting down large trees with a chain saw was inherently dangerous, and the stretch of turnpike Partridge traveled twice a day was also dangerous, claiming a couple of dozen lives a year. So there was nothing unusual about the accidents, and their happening so close together was pure coincidence.

His conscience clear and his mood upbeat, Harry decided to do some work and began by checking his email. The first message he opened was from a curator at the museum to which he had emailed a picture of the souvenir statuette for identification:

*Your statuette is a representation of Iktel, a deity of the Kogi civilization that inhabited Northern Columbia until the fifteenth century. The Kogis venerated Iktel as a protector and would propitiate him with offerings so he would vanquish their foes. They also feared him, believing he would become vindictive toward them if he felt underappreciated or disrespected. "Iktel" means "crusher," which is why he is depicted with his fists pressed together and his teeth bared. If you care to bring the piece in, I would be happy to opine on its authenticity.*

---

Two days later the Curator sat behind his desk scrutinizing the statuette with a magnifying glass.

"It looks authentic, although I'll have to run some tests to be certain. You're sure you want to donate it?"

"Yes, I'm sure," Harry said. "I've come to realize it needs—is entitled to, special care."

"Where did you get it?"

"In Cartagena, Columbia, about ten days ago. Cartagena was a port-of-call on a cruise that my wife and I took. I bought it from a pushcart vendor in the old part of the city. Paid two hundred US dollars for it because he insisted it was an original, though I didn't believe him. He put it in a bag with a large silk flower and warned it would be bad luck not to keep them together. Made a big thing of it."

"Are you superstitious?" the Curator asked, looking amused.

Not wanting to seem a fool, Harry had decided in advance not to mention the two accidents.

"Well, I didn't suffer any ill effects after I discarded the silk flower when we got home. But you could say I compensated for it by putting the statuette on a shelf overlooking a vase my wife keeps filled with fresh ones."

The Curator chuckled and held up the gallon-sized storage bag filled with fresh flowers that Harry had transported the statuette in. "So you're not taking any chances."

"Right."

"Well, good. That means both sides get something out of this transaction—the Museum, an addition to its collection, and you, relief from anxiety."

"Yeah, reciprocity," Harry said, sounding weary.

The Curator filled out a receipt, handed it to Harry, they shook hands, and Harry left. As soon as the door closed, the Curator made a phone call.

"It's the real thing all right. A gorgeous piece, and there'll be no risk in keeping it. Columbia has too many problems on its plate to care about Kogi artifacts. I'll bring it right down."

He wrapped the statuette in cotton and placed it in a small cardboard box.

"No more flowers for you," he said imperiously, as he tossed the freezer bag into a trash can.

His destination was an office ten floors below, and he was eager to get there. So he decided to gamble on a nearby staff elevator that had been performing erratically as of late.

*"The vulnerability in being stranded alone in the middle of the Maine woods after dark."*

# THE MISFITS

"It is unpleasant to go alone,
even to be drowned."
Russian Proverb

Adam was slowly driving his SUV along a narrow woodland road under a star-splattered northern sky. He spotted a small dirt parking area for hikers and hunters, pulled into it, cut the engine, and climbed out.

---

Something large suddenly appeared in her high beams. Being on Moose-alert, she flinched and started to brake before realizing what it was—an SUV parked in a small roadside clearing with its lights on and a man standing alongside. Recognizing the vulnerability in being stranded alone in the middle of the Maine woods after dark, she pulled over be-hind the SUV. She saw the man was young and was removing his shirt.

"If you're planning to sunbathe, your timing is a bit off," she joked with her warmest smile as she approached him.

He chuckled politely. "Not quite, but I'm okay and don't need help, so you can just keep going. And thanks for stopping."

*An odd reaction*, she thought. She was beautiful and seductively dressed in tight jeans and T-shirt. She walked to within arms-length of him, and, in the light of the SUV's taillights, scrutinized his face, which was handsome, and his torso, which was well muscled.

"What's your name?" she asked.

"Adam, but please go."

"You're very good looking, Adam. How about kissing me?" She said this while placing a hand on his shoulder and moving her face toward his.

He pushed her hand away angrily. "For god's sake, leave me alone and get the hell out of here! I mean it."

She gave him a puzzled look and then laughed softly.

"I'm not going to do that Adam. You see, I have a rare condition, and there's an element in human blood that I need to ingest periodically in order to stay alive and healthy. So I really need your help."

He took a deep breath, got his exasperation under control, and smiled patiently.

"I get it and it's very funny, Miss…"

"Evelyn," she interjected.

"It's very funny, Evelyn, and you're a beautiful girl. Even though hookers aren't my thing, I'd be tempted to make an exception in your case. But there's something really, really important I have to do right now and I have to do it alone. So I'm begging you, please go."

"Don't believe me, huh?" She stooped and effortlessly lifted a very large slab of granite, balanced it on one hand, and hurled it deep into the woods. The sound of splintering tree trunks testified to the awesome power behind the throw. Then she smiled, and Adam saw her incisors and canines slowly extend and retract. He stood transfixed by astonishment and horror.

"So come and give me a kiss, Adam. It's kind of like making love. You surrender, I'll be gentle, and you'll find it very satisfying."

"This is totally absurd," he exclaimed shrilly. "I was trying to protect you from me, and now I'm the one needing protection. Listen to me, Evelyn. I'm wolfenspawn, a werewolf. My blood can't be good for you. It's not normal blood.

"And," he added desperately, "there must be some kind of professional courtesy that applies here."

She was delighted by this and laughed. "You really are very funny, Adam, and it was a good try, but I'm afraid the wolfen died out long ago."

"You're wrong. Just give me ten minutes and I'll prove it," he pleaded. "As soon as the moon comes up, you'll see for yourself."

She pondered this and glanced at the sky. *He's probably just a neo-Druid out for some kind of full-moon ritual, but I suppose I ought to make sure*, she thought.

"All right, but turn off your lights and let's walk a ways into the woods."

"I was going to do that anyway," he said testily, as he removed the rest of his clothing, except for his boxer shorts, and placed it in the SUV.

They followed a narrow trail through the trees for several minutes until they came to a large clearing in which a dozen tall blocks of granite were arranged Stonehenge style around the remains of a large fire.

Evelyn sniggered as she thought, *A Druid setup for sure. He probably has a ceremonial robe in the SUV. More of them may be coming and I only want one, so I'd better take him soon.*

Adam squatted near the remains of the fire, and Evelyn leaned against a granite block watching him carefully, expecting him to bolt into the woods any second.

"Do you come here often?" she asked.

"Never before. I stopped where I did because there was room to park off the road. This looks like a meeting place for a Wicca coven."

"You belong to one?"

"No, though I looked into Wicca and other neo-pagan and Native American religions to see if there was a cure for my problem. They had nothing."

Adam seemed so calm and relaxed that Evelyn began to wonder whether he was telling the truth after all.

"How did you come to be wolfen?"

"It's in my family's genes. Skips some generations but not mine obviously. My parents saw signs when I was about twelve and prepared me for it. You know, 'be sure to get deep into the woods on the first night of the full moon.' That kind of thing."

"Sounds like you've got it under control."

"Usually. But tonight I got stuck at work and wasn't able to get to the cabin. I have a cabin deep in the woods."

"So you have a job. Are you married, or do you have a girlfriend?"

"No. Can't afford to let anyone get close if I don't want to end up as a freak in a science lab."

"Must be a lonely life."

"Well, I have some friends, though no close ones. But, yeah, it's lonely compared with the relationships other people have. Particularly since my parents died. I could open up to them."

She nodded sympathetically, knowing what it was like not to have anyone to unburden to.

"Look, I'm starting to change!" he said pointing to a thick gray stubble that now covered his torso and limbs. "You can see in the dark, right?" When she answered "yes" he turned away from her before removing his boxer shorts.

Evelyn couldn't remember when she had last been the object of a chivalrous gesture and was touched.

A few hundred feet beyond the clearing a twig snapped.

"Do you usually make a kill?" she asked.

"Yeah, deer mostly, but sometimes humans cross my path and, well, I can't help myself. I feel sick when I think about it the next day. What about you?"

For reasons she didn't understand the question made her uncomfortable, and she minimized her body count. "One a month is all I really need. I'd like to say I only choose people the world is better off without, but appearances can be deceiving, and I move around too much to get to know who's who, though I enjoy talking with people and do as much socializing as I can, which isn't much."

"Move around?"

"From city to city, hotel to hotel."

"Where do you get the money to support yourself?"

"Burglary, which comes easy to me as you can probably imagine. If I didn't move I'd become a one-woman crime wave before long."

"I thought you couldn't enter a home unless you are invited."

"Early in the evening I go door-to-door selling magazines for charity. If the man of the house answers, I usually get in. Then I return much later when they are asleep."

"You operate alone then?"

She nodded. "Clans and even couples are impractical if you want to stay under the radar. So I'm even more isolated than you are."

"You must be very, very…must have lived a long time."

She laughed. "Yes, but my body is young and that's what counts. Oh, I know what you're thinking. But it's a real body, not an illusion. If I were to be killed I'd leave behind a dead young woman not a pile of ashes."

"It's coming on fast," Adam said. He was on his hands and knees now, and Evelyn watched with interest as his torso lengthened and limbs reshaped themselves, grateful that when she chose to shapeshift it happened instantaneously.

Then she surprised herself by blurting, "How about we meet for dinner tomorrow night? In Portland at Barry's Steak House at eight?"

"Love…to," Adam managed to squeeze out with difficulty just before his larynx changed.

"Fantastic. Still, if you don't mind, I'll stay with you a while longer tonight."

But her words were drowned out in Adam's ears by a loud buzzing sound accompanying a hot surge that flowed through his body. Suddenly he felt powerful, fast, and hungry. He looked down at where his hands had rested and saw large gray paws. The change was complete. He tilted his head back and howled rapturously at the moon, and then started in surprise when an answering call came immediately from close behind. He turned to see a young she-wolf standing alongside a granite pillar and looking his way. She was the most magnificent creature he had ever seen, and she was in heat.

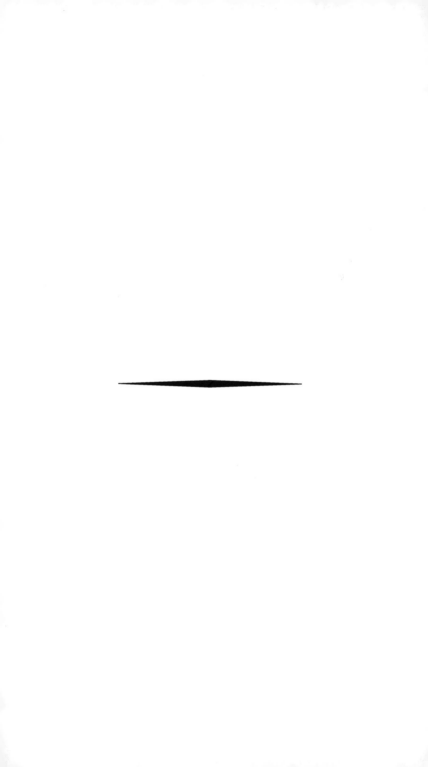

*"Butch watched with a sad and puzzled
expression as the car pulled away."*

# THE WHOLE TRUTH

"Follow not truth too near the heels,
lest it dash out thy teeth."
George Herbert

As the Boeing 747 began its descent to Haneda International Airport, Dave Richards realized he had left home without his hearing aids. He did well enough without them in most situations, but always wore them to important business meetings like the one he was about to attend in Tokyo.

This blunder seemed all of a piece with the way his life had been going. Sales to his accounts were down sixty percent, and he expected his employer, Argis Technologies, to include him in its next round of downsizing.

In contrast, his wife Penelope was rapidly scaling the ladder of success at a large investment house. Since her latest promotion a month earlier, they had spent little time together and had had no sex. Penny stayed at the office until nine, worked weekends, and when at home was in continual smartphone contact with Bruce, her boss and mentor. Dave was jealous and, try as he might, he could not avoid the painful suspicion that they were sleeping together. After all, it was Penny's beauty that had distinguished her from the equally bright and hardworking female colleagues who were passed over for the promotion.

Dave's meeting that day was with Ichi Noda, head of software purchasing for Yokohama Electronics, his biggest account. Twenty-four hours earlier Noda had asked him to come to Tokyo as soon as possible. So there he was, tired, jet lagged, and wrinkled with only fifty minutes to get to the meeting. Because it was critical that he follow everything Noda said, he desperately hoped he could buy a pair of one-size-fits-all hearing aids at the airport. When he asked a security guard about this, he was directed to an electronics kiosk in the airport's Rashomon Gate food court.

The wizened old man behind the kiosk counter said all he had was a super high-tech model that had been manufactured in Japan for the Israeli army. He produced a pair for Dave's inspection.

"My God, they're green. I can't wear these."

"Make for army," he reminded Dave irritably, and then produced a smaller pair that would fit entirely within the ear and be out of sight. Dave tried them and found the clarity to be astounding. Still he was shocked when the old man wanted $15,000 US for the pair.

"Very advanced. Very secret. Jew army use for terrorist. Find lies. Cough two times for on and two times for off."

Dave laughed and said he wanted hearing aids not lie detectors, and $15,000 was much too high.

"If I shop around Tokyo, I'll find them for a third the price," he said, hoping to get him down to around $8,000, which would be ballpark reasonable for a pair of high quality hearing aids.

"No, believe me you no find. I exclusive. Fall off back of truck. Understand?"

Dave had no time to shop, and the meeting with Noda was important, so he caved and bought them with a credit card. He asked for an instruction manual, and the old man scowled and mumbled as he rummaged through a drawer. Then he found what he was looking for and, with a beatific smile, handed Dave a small booklet written in Hebrew.

The meeting with Noda took place in a large, simply furnished conference room with about fifteen non-participating onlookers present, presumably all subordinates of Noda eager to learn at the feet of their master. The great man, who did not speak English, told Dave through Ms. Joji, his modern dressed but geisha-like assistant, that he owed him an apology. He said he had invited Dave to Tokyo intending to pleasantly surprise him by purchasing

Argis's Erda 2 software for all of Yokohama's assembly plants. But an hour earlier he had unexpectedly received a report from Yokohama's testing laboratory concluding that the Cobra software produced by Atman-Gita Ltd., an Indian firm, was the equal of Erda 2.

"Mr. Noda extremely regretful he now cannot buy Erda because Cobra license fee much, much lower," Ms. Joji said sadly, and then presented Dave with a consolation prize—a large gift-wrapped box, which he later found to contain a very expensive vase.

This was not like any negotiation Dave had ever been a part of before. He slowly poured and drank a glass of water to gain time to collect his thoughts before responding. Some of the water went down the wrong way, he coughed twice, and the hearing aids chirped a signal into his ears. *Okay*, he thought, *let's see what these $15,000 suckers can do.*

"Ms. Joji, did I understand Mr. Noda to say that, according to Yokohama Labs, Erda is not at all superior to Cobra?"

She translated the question, and Noda said something in Japanese that the hearing aids indicated was a lie. "Yes, Erda no better than Cobra," she told him.

Feeling empowered by the knowledge that Yokohama Labs considered Erda the better product and knowing that Noda wanted it badly, given the Japanese obsession with quality, Dave stood up and delivered the biggest line of bullshit of his life.

"Ms. Joji, please tell Mr. Noda that my sorrow about his decision almost overwhelms me. This is not because my company has lost a very important sale, which it truly has. No, the reason that I'm so deeply saddened is because today marks the end of Argis's relationship with Yokohama Electronics, a firm it holds in the highest esteem. I wish we could match Atman-Gita's price, but that is not possible. You see in order to be sure we would retain your business, we priced Erda 2 for you with such a razor thin profit margin that it required a special approval from our board of directors. The approval was granted only because the board believed the eminence of Yokohama Electronics rubbed off on Argis by association. Their disappointment and sorrow will be very, very great."

Dave knew Noda didn't have a sentimental bone in his body and did not expect him to swallow any of this. And he was not surprised that Noda and everyone else present were well mannered enough to give the appearance of being moved. The important thing was he had given Noda cover to change his mind without losing face. And change it he did, after leaving the room to consult with his upper management for three-quarters of an hour. His lying explanation for the reversal was that money was not the most important thing, and a price could not be put on trust, loyalty, and friendship between companies.

This was an amazing result considering that Argis was willing to cut the license fee in half to win the contract. Dave was eager to spread the news but, because of the time zone difference, had to wait until the morning.

Ms. Joji, who was strikingly beautiful, approached him after the meeting and said she'd love to show him around Tokyo anytime he liked. He would have enjoyed her company, but her enthusiasm was feigned and the offer was probably Noda's idea, so he did not pursue it.

Over a solitary dinner, Dave daydreamed of triumphs achieved through the "gremlins," which was what he called the tiny green hearing aids. True, there would be a limited window of opportunity before the technology became generally known and a neutralizing device were developed. But if he played his cards right and moved quickly there would be enough time to set himself up for a happy and financially secure future. The fact that he was unable at that point to come up with even a general plan of action did not bother him. He was sure he would do better after he returned home and caught up on his sleep.

When he called Penny's office the next morning her secretary said she was at an important meeting and could not come to the phone, and the gremlins signaled "lie." But this did not bother him. She was probably frantically working to meet a deadline and had told her secretary to block all calls. He had no trouble getting through to his boss who congratulated him heartily without meaning it. Dave guessed he had already submitted his name for the next round of layoffs and would now look foolish reversing himself.

The next evening he arrived home to an empty house at about eight. Penny was still at work and his special pal Butch, a wirehaired fox terrier, was at a boarding kennel. Penny got in an hour later looking tired but beautiful and sexy. After pouring two glasses of wine, he gave her a blow-by-blow account of his triumph, but without diminishing it by mentioning the gremlins.

When he finished she rewarded him with a passionate kiss but then spoiled it by suggesting they postpone celebrating until the weekend because she was totally burned out. This made him angry. She had been dodging sex with him for weeks, and he was at that moment feeling especially randy because of his triumph in Tokyo.

"You know, Pen, if I didn't know you better I'd figure your late hours and lack of libido mean you're sleeping with Bruce."

She exploded. "How dare you suggest that! I'm not cheating on you and never would. But what I will do is leave you if you ever accuse me again."

To his horror, the gremlins signaled she was lying. Stunned, he did not know what to say or do.

Back at the office, everyone offered Dave smiling but insincere congratulations on his success in Tokyo. He attributed their hypocrisy, as well as the universal dislike for him that he began to perceive, to jealousy. This was especially hurtful because he was accustomed to considering himself well liked. He had always gotten along with everyone, frequently made people laugh, and often offered a helping hand to a colleague in need. But to hell with them all, he decided. With the help of Japanese and Israeli technology he would become the company's top negotiator, move up in rank, and forget he ever knew them.

And it unfolded exactly as he hoped. Mindful of his stunning success in Tokyo, upper management asked him to join long deadlocked negotiations with the labor union representing their technicians. Two weeks later the company achieved a favorable settlement by following Dave's bold advice to call the union's bluff by saying theirs was a take-it-or-leave-it offer and walking away from the bargaining table. He was promptly rewarded with a promotion, raise, larger office, and trophy secretary.

But he was not happy, and Penny's unfaithfulness and his co-workers' hypocrisy were not the only reasons. He had found that he had to limit his use of the gremlins because, unless he was alone with the TV and radio turned off, they chirped continuously. This meant he was in the midst of a sea of lies and deceit, and his lifelong belief in fundamental human decency was a myth.

One evening when Dave had been out drinking heavily alone, he absentmindedly returned home with the gremlins in their detection mode. He was shocked to hear them signal "lie" when the dog affectionately greeted him at the door with the usual enthusiastic barking, jumping, and tail wagging. So there it was. Butch didn't care a fig for him personally and was just cajoling him for food and a walk. Living with one deceiver was more than enough, so he took the dog for a ride and let him out of the car on the shoulder of an eight-lane expressway. Butch watched with a sad and puzzled expression as the car pulled away.

Dave awoke the next morning realizing that in his drunken state he had made a horrible mistake: the gremlins were designed to process human speech, not canine barking and yelping, and he had put his only true friend in harm's way. Finding that Butch had not returned, he hurriedly dressed and drove to the drop-off point where he called and whistled into the adjacent woods without success. It took another hour of searching before he spotted the dog's lifeless body lying in an exit ramp less than a mile from home. He pulled onto the shoulder and wept.

———

Penny continued to devote all her time and energy to her job, and they seldom spoke. Once, in an effort to dispel the tension between them, she said she loved him, and he just needed to be patient while she went through a high-pressure probationary period in her new job. Dave would have been happy to believe that, but the gremlins signaled "lie," and he attributed the overture to fear that he would ruin her career by filing for divorce on grounds of adultery with her boss.

Because he vaguely hoped for an end to her affair and a reconciliation, he let matters drift. But then the dreams began—vivid, tormenting ones in which Penny gave herself to Bruce in various erotic scenarios that mirrored her real-life love making with Dave in happier times. Gradually his vague hope morphed into unequivocal hatred.

According to the eminent seventh century Christian theologian Augustine of Hippo, sexual attraction is the Deity's punishment of humankind for Adam and Eve's Original Sin. Centuries later Shakespeare wrote the great tragedy in which sexual jealousy destroys Othello and Desdemona. And in our own time there is the scientific finding that all of the great apes, including humans, are programmed to compete for mates and to crave vengeance when victimized.

So it was hardly surprising that Dave was elated when an opportunity to settle the score with Penny finally came in the form of a long-planned vacation in Maine. Penny readily agreed to go even though she was very busy at work. She was well aware of the hostility Dave was feeling and saw the short vacation as an opportunity to focus on him and put their relationship back on an even keel.

Dave had spent days carefully planning her murder, but during the drive north his conscience began chipping away at his resolve.

*Maybe Bruce is forcing her to have sex, exploiting her ambition. She may hate what she's doing.*

*Oh yeah. Well, not in the dreams I'm having.*

*But dreams are just dreams.*

*Come on. If it were sexual harassment she'd blow the whistle on him.*

*And jeopardize her career? She might not be believed.*

Dave knew he needed to act fast or not at all. So as soon as they arrived at their motel he checked the marine weather forecast and then proposed they work up an appetite for dinner by paddling their kayak to an uninhabited island three miles from shore. He knew that the twenty-knot winds forecast together with tidal conditions would produce high seas. When they got to the launch site in a small, protected harbor, he told Penny he had forgotten to pack their life vests and convinced her they could safely leave without them even though she was a poor swimmer. He held the double kayak steady as she climbed into the front cockpit and then climbed into the rear one from which he operated the foot pedals that controlled the rudder. They stretched the bottoms of their spray skirts over the cockpit mouths, tightened them around their waists, and paddled for the harbor mouth.

As they entered the bay, they were greeted by a near gale-force wind, and a sea covered with fierce looking white caps. Penny turned to him from the front cockpit, looking terrified, and said something he could not hear over the howling of the wind.

"It's okay," he shouted. "We just have to keep our bow into the waves. On the return trip the wind will be at our back. It'll be easy."

Two-thirds of the way to the island he turned the kayak abeam to a five-foot wave, and it flipped over. He worked himself free from the spray skirt that held him in the cockpit and got to the surface with the help of a partially inflated snorkeling vest he wore hidden under his jacket. The boat slowly drifted away from him with Penny stuck in the cockpit underwater. All he had to do was stay afloat while the outgoing tide carried him to the island and wait to be rescued.

But then he imagined her struggling underwater and expecting him to save her, and could not go through with it. He swam to the overturned kayak, reached underneath, got a grip on one of her arms, and, bracing his feet on the side of the boat, frantically pulled and pulled until she came free. She was not conscious, and he wrapped his arms around her and kicked his legs to keep their heads above water. At the same time he squeezed her as hard as he could, hoping it would help her cough up any water in her lungs.

But he was soon near the point of exhaustion where the only way to save himself would be to let her sink. Then he saw they were drifting close to a group of rocks, and he expended the last of his energy in reaching them. He wedged Penny in a gap between two boulders, and, after resting half a minute, managed to get them both onto the rocks and out of the water. He checked Penny's wrist for a pulse and thought he detected a faint one. Because of the howling wind and crashing waves, he could not tell whether she was breathing. He performed mouth-to-mouth resuscitation, but she didn't revive. Then he remembered hypothermia and lay on top of her to transfer heat from his body to hers. He talked to her to keep her brain active—begging her not to give up and promising to always love her no matter what she did, even if she wanted to leave him.

Half an hour later they were spotted by a passing lobster boat which radioed for help. The police harbor patrol picked them up, wrapped them both in blankets, and put an oxygen mask on Penny. When they arrived at the hospital Dave insisted he was okay and would not be separated from her. He was holding her hand when the ER doctor pronounced her dead.

"I did all I could to save her," he said, sobbing. "I gave her mouth-to-mouth, tried to keep her warm."

"Don't blame yourself, Mr. Richards. She had drowned by the time you got her to the surface."

Dave gave a policeman a brief account of what happened, and then returned to his motel room where the sight of Penny's unpacked suitcase pierced his heart. He told himself over and over that she deserved to die because she had betrayed him and her sacred marriage vows. But he found peace only when he had drunk himself senseless at a local pub whose patrons carried him back to his room at closing time.

The next morning a detective named Carney and his partner, Smith, came to see him. They apologized for intruding on his grief and explained that because of the loss of life they could not postpone fleshing out the very short statement he had given the evening before.

Dave was startled to see that both of them were wearing green hearing aids.

"I see you have those lie detector hearing aids the Japanese made for the Israelis. I bought a pair on the black market while on business in Tokyo."

"Yeah, True-Finds, they're great," Carney said. "We just got them as part of an FBI sponsored trial. But you have it backwards. The technology detects speech frequencies associated with sincerity. It turns out this is better than lie detection because it can't be faked."

Dave's gremlins signaled Carney was lying, but he couldn't understand why he would.

Smith chuckled. "You may owe some people an apology if you've been treating them like liars because of the True-Finds. Hope you didn't do anything drastic."

"No, nothing drastic," Dave said.

He saw them exchange puzzled glances, and hastily added, "If you don't count killing my dog."

They laughed heartily, and Dave forced a smile, while tucking his hands under his legs so they would not see he was trembling.

*"They'd save a lot of money if they
hired some Zuni rain dancers."*

# LOVE AMIDST GLOBAL WARMING

I was three weeks into the around-the-world cruise on which I was employed as a pianist. It was my first time as a cruise ship musician and I was liking it a lot. The food was good, my room was small but pleasant, and my job was easy, consisting of playing background music in the various cocktail lounges scattered around the huge ship. I was allowed to play whatever I liked so long as it didn't interfere with the conversation and drinking, which was not difficult with people accustomed to listening to iPods while multitasking.

But best of all, I had become friends with the four lovely and bright Russian women comprising the ship's classical string quartet, most especially with Yuliya, the viola player.

The only negative aspect of my job was having to spend three months in what was essentially an enormous floating resort that dumped over a hundred thousand gallons of sewage into the ocean daily, and continuously spewed toxic emissions from the tons of dirty bunker fuel burned by its giant engines. To ease my conscience I had made a generous donation to Oceana, the international ocean conservation organization, before I left.

After passing through the Panama Canal, we stopped at Acapulco for a day and then cruised up the coast to San Francisco where we docked overnight. The musicians got shore leave, and I went with the quartet when they played at a luncheon banquet given in their honor by Tatyana the cellist's relatives. Afterward Yuliya and I went to visit my Grandmother in a new Chevy sedan that Tatyana's cousin, Ilya, insisted on lending me. I was ecstatic when Yuliya wanted to come. We had been keeping our emotional cards close to our chests so she couldn't know I adored her, and I had no idea whether her feelings for me went beyond friendship. Her choosing a visit to my grandmother's over a tour of beautiful San Francisco was encouraging.

Gram lived three hours from the city in an imposing Victorian farmhouse that was a local landmark. It sat, surrounded by thirsty-looking grass and shrubs, on a half-acre plot adjacent to a gated community that was built on land that my great-great-grandfather had once farmed.

I knew Gram had taken an immediate liking to Yuliya when, bad hip notwithstanding, she gave her a grand tour of the charming old house. During dinner out on the front porch, Gram continued down memory lane, entertaining us with happy stories her mother told about growing up on the farm.

Yuliya was delighted.

"It sounds like she had a wonderful childhood. Why did the family stop farming?"

"The real estate just became too valuable not to sell," I offered.

"Yes, there was that," Gram said. "But mainly it was the lack of rain. This valley was kind of freakish and had always been extremely dry until my grandfather, Poppy Ian, arrived. Locals thought him a fool for trying to farm here, but as soon as he started the weather changed and stayed that way until he died."

"So it rained more?" Yuliya asked, seeming pleased.

Gram nodded. "People joked that he brought it with him from the Aran Islands, that's where he was from, but our family has always kind of believed that in fact he did. A climate researcher at the University who I consulted years ago checked the records and confirmed there was a significant increase in rainfall during Poppy's farming years. I asked if there was a scientific explanation for it and he said 'not really.' He said that precipitation in the valley is dependent on cloud formation, which in turn is a function of two factors. One is topography, which of course didn't change while Poppy was farming. The other factor is the movement of the atmosphere, which is caused by radiation from the sun. This must have changed locally, though he couldn't say why. And, you know, I recently read in a newspaper article that predicting how cloud patterns will change is still the biggest uncertainty in weather forecasting and the greatest remaining mystery in climate science."

"Well, I don't see any mystery in what happened," I said. "The logical explanation is that Poppy Ian moved to the valley at the right time and was the lucky beneficiary of a very early manifestation of global warming, or 'global weirding' as some scientists call it."

But Yuliya was not inclined to dismiss the mystical. "I think it's just as likely that he did bring the rain. The Slavic people have always believed it possible. There is an ancient ritual called 'Dodola' that they still perform in some places during a drought."

Gram, who had obviously done her homework, jumped on the Twilight Zone bandwagon. "The Zuni and other Southwest American Indians tribes have rain-making rituals too. And there are all those Christian saints who could bring the rains: Swithin in England, Medard in France, Godelieve in Belgium. And in India a Sufi Muslim holy man, Baba Dhokal, could do it. Poppy Ian was religious and probably prayed for rain."

I was, and still am, a firm believer in the adage that if you can't beat 'em you should join 'em. So I said, with a grin I couldn't suppress, "Well, there may be something to it then. I really need to find out whether I inherited Poppy Ian's rain- making powers. I could give up music and make big bucks working for the government or for private industry."

"You inherited Poppy's musical talent, and that should be enough for you, smart aleck," Gram snapped.

I knew that Yuliya loved Tolstoy, and that he idealized cultured farmers. So I wasn't surprised by her reaction.

"Ah, a farmer-musician! How wonderful! What instrument did he play?"

"The concertina. He played Irish and Scottish airs and also waltzes and jigs that we would dance to."

I explained to Yuliya that Celtic airs were song-like tunes without words, but she already knew this.

"We played some on a cruise that stopped at Ireland and Scotland. I liked them a lot."

Gram got to her feet. "I have one of Poppy's music books. My sister had it until she died last year. I'll get it."

She returned with a slender volume with yellowed pages and a crumbling binding. The tattered cover bore a drawing of a rocky island being assaulted by pounding surf and the title "Ancient Airs of the Isles." She handled the book gingerly, as though it were the Book of Kells, and paged through it until she found the tune she was looking for.

"This one, 'Cape Far,' was his favorite. They had an accordionist play it while they scattered his ashes in the ocean."

Yuliya glanced at me and, reading her mind, I went to fetch her viola from the car.

When I returned she was studying the music.

"There's no tempo marking, but it has lots of lilting dotted eighth notes, so adagio I think."

I handed her the viola, and she checked the tuning and began to play.

There is a special joy for a musician in playing unknown music out of curiosity and finding it to be beautiful. And so Yuliya, who was serious most of the time and always when she performed, was smiling gently as she played.

The piece was wordless only in the sense that it had no lyrics. But the images and emotions it evoked were wonderfully articulate, speaking of sky and wind, of sea and cliffs, of wild flowers tenuously clinging to barren crags, of hard work by fishermen trolling the ocean and farmers tilling the soil, of loneliness, of love, and, most emphatically, of the nobility of it all.

She played Cape Far again with an improvised drone background that made it even more moving. Then she played several of the other airs in the book, each of which was lovely in a different way. A beautiful woman playing beautiful music. My heart was melting.

Afterward Gram painstaking photocopied the book for Yuliya, served up coffee and scones to fortify us for the drive back, and, while we enjoyed them, attempted, not very subtly, to elicit information about the depth of our relationship.

So after asking Yuliya about her family and learning that her parents lived in Kiev in the Ukraine, she turned to me: "I'll bet Kiev is a fascinating place to visit with lots of history. Do you think you'll get to see it someday?"

The sun was just starting to set as she walked us to the car. I could hear the whir of the sprinkler systems watering the lawns and trees in the gated community.

"They'd save a lot of money if they hired some Zuni rain dancers," I almost wisecracked, but held my tongue.

"I hope you'll both come visit me again sometime," Gram said, emphasizing the word "both" and looking me sternly in the eye.

I pretended to have missed the don't-let-this-girl-get-away message.

"Sure, Gram, and maybe someday by chance we'll bump into each other in Kiev."

It took her a moment to realize I was teasing, and then she laughed, and Yuliya and I did too.

The drive back to San Francisco was heavenly. Because Ilya had selected the optional three-passenger front seat for his sedan, Yuliya was able to choose the middle position and sit close to me rather than near the window as she had done earlier. She had skipped the coffee and about ten minutes into the trip fell sound asleep with her head resting on my shoulder. Thrilled by the warmth of her body and the smell of her hair, I didn't mind having to slow down when it started to rain.

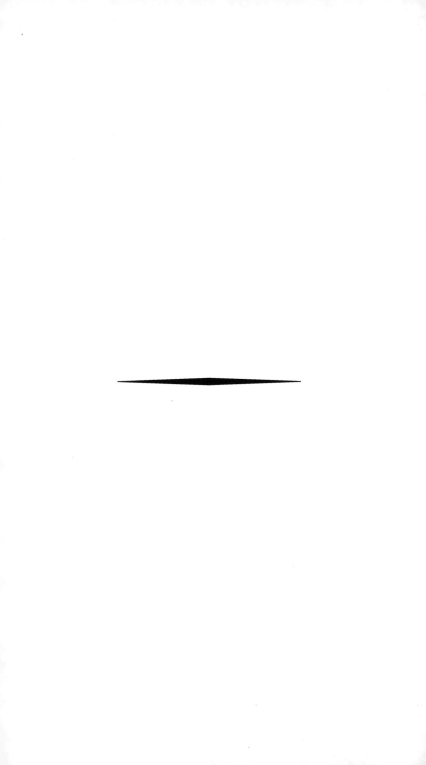

*"The apocryphal books of the old Testament
say that demons are fallen angels."*

# THE APPRENTICE

Paul Redford, a slender, distinguished looking man dressed in a black suit, white shirt, and black tie, sat at his desk waiting for the arrival of clients Sam and Mary Buckley and their twenty-three-year-old daughter, Brenna. When a buzzer signaled their entrance into his waiting room, Redford, who could not afford a secretary, greeted them himself and ushered them into the office.

They seated themselves around a conference table, and Sam Buckley, who looked disgruntled, was the first to speak.

"Before we start, I'd like Mr. Redford to tell me what his qualifications are for this kind of thing."

"I already told you, Dad," his daughter said, exasperated.

"It's okay, Brenna, I'm happy to oblige," Redford said and turned to Buckley.

"I've earned doctorates in theology and psychology from Yale, I'm a member in good standing of two theological societies, and I'm licensed to provide psychological counseling. I've been a practicing psychologist for eleven years, specializing in religion-related mental illness and family disputes. And to bring things up-to-date, I'm meeting with you folks today about your daughter's upcoming same-sex marriage."

Redford's cell phone emitted a siren-like ring tone.

"I'm sorry, I have to take this. It's my signal for emergencies." He left the room and returned two minutes later.

"That was the police department's hostage negotiator. A teenager tried to rob a liquor store and is inside now with three hostages. They want me to get over there right away."

"Why do the need you?" Buckley asked.

"The boy's mother claims he's not responsible for his actions because he's possessed by a demon."

———

Party Hour Liquors occupied all of a one-story cinder block building that sat in the middle of an asphalt parking lot. Five police cars with policemen behind them were fanned out in a semicircle in front of the store. Behind them a satellite truck and TV crew from the Jackal Network waited at the curb for the outcome.

Redford parked behind the truck and walked to where Lieutenant Bill Rizzo, a short, stocky man with Italianate features, was waiting for him with a middle-aged Latino woman.

"Thanks for getting here so quickly, Doc. We don't have a lot of time. This is Mrs. Cruz, the perpetrator's mother. His name is Hector."

"How do you do, Mrs. Cruz. I'm very sorry about your trouble. Please tell me why you think Hector is possessed by a demon."

"I hear him talking to it, and he was a good boy before then."

"Does he take any kind of medication or use drugs?"

"No, never."

"Have you ever heard him address the demon by name?"

Rizzo laughed. "You gonna want me to see if it has a record?"

"Not quite. Exorcism is supposed to be more effective when you have the name."

"Hector never say a name," Mrs. Cruz said. "I don't know, but last month he put 'Bethany' on his arm. You know, tattoo. He don't know no Bethany. His girlfriend is Luisa."

"We really need to hurry, Doc," Rizzo said. "Want anything else from Mrs. Cruz?"

Redford shook his head, and Rizzo told a female cop to wait with Mrs. Cruz in a patrol car parked across the street in front of the sawhorse barricades the police were using to contain the onlookers.

Redford removed a book from his briefcase and opened it to a place he had marked with a scrap of paper.

"I'm ready, Lieutenant. I'll leave my case with you so he'll see I'm unarmed."

"You're not going inside, Doc. We've been negotiating with him on the phone, and you can do it that way. Exorcise him over the phone."

"This is ridiculous."

"I know, but go through the motions for the mother's sake. I want her to feel we've done everything possible to avoid hurting her son, especially if we kill him."

Rizzo dialed.

"Hi, Hector. This is Bill Rizzo again. We are still considering your demands, and we'll have an answer in a couple of minutes. In the meantime, I'd like you to talk to a friend of your mother's."

He handed the phone to Redford.

"Hello, Hector. My name is Paul Redford. I'm a theologian. I have just been talking with your mother, and she wants me to read you a prayer that may help you in your current situation. Will you listen?"

"Go ahead," he said with an exaggerated gruffness that was obviously intended to mask his fear.

Redford took a deep breath and began reading the concluding section of an ancient Roman Catholic rite of exorcism, which was the only one he had been able to find. Where it said "Satan" he substituted "Bethany."

"Depart, Bethany, seducer, full of lies and cunning, foe of virtue, persecutor of the innocent. Give place, abominable creature, give way, you monster, give way to Christ, in whom you found none of your works. For he has already stripped you of your powers and laid waste your kingdom, bound you prisoner and plundered your weapons. He has cast you forth into outer darkness, where everlasting ruin awaits you and your abettors."

He heard a clunk from Hector's end.

"Sounds like he dropped the phone."

Rizzo raised his arm and five heavily armed cops wearing swat team gear charged into the store. A minute later one of them emerged and yelled to Rizzo, "The hostages are okay. We found the kid on the floor unconscious."

"Son of a bitch," Rizzo said, "your mumbo jumbo worked."

The TV crew moved in and a handsome man with a mike proceeded to interview Redford. His introduction showed that Jackal had done some quick research.

"I have with me Doctor Paul Redford, a Theologian Psychologist, and the author of 'Religion as a Cause of Mental Illness.'"

The mention of the book pleased Redford. Only 610 of them had been sold. His agent was so desperate for publicity, he had sent free copies to radical Muslim organizations in hopes someone would issue a fatwa condemning Redford to death.

"Doctor Redford, is it true that you just performed an exorcism on the gunman?"

"Well, it's true that I performed the rite of exorcism. But by definition there's no exorcism unless a demon is present and expelled."

He was about to attribute Hector's loss of consciousness to the placebo effect when he noticed that a woman standing behind the reporter, probably his producer, was shaking her head in disapproval. He got her point. He was brushing aside the mystical possibilities that would make the story prime time material on the sensationalist Jackal Evening News. So he changed tack.

"However, his mother is convinced he was possessed, and he did in fact collapse after I read the prayer, so maybe she was right. We'll have to wait and see if his behavior changes."

"Aren't exorcisms usually performed by clergymen?"

"Yes. Some priests are authorized by their bishops to perform them, but there wasn't time to find one."

"What kinds of things did the demon make the gunman do besides rob stores?"

"A better person to answer that would be Lieutenant Rizzo here."

The reporter put the mike in front of Rizzo, and Redford walked across the street to Mrs. Cruz to give her what comfort he could. She hugged him when he said he was willing to appear without fee as an expert witness on the issue of Hector's mental capacity. But Redford was not motivated by charity alone. He expected Hector's lawyer to use a demonic possession defense that would attract nationwide media attention.

A fortyish woman dressed in slacks, turtle neck sweater, and black leather zipper jacket joined them. She reminded Redford of the kind of actress who played a tough cop in a TV series.

"Hello, Doctor Redford. I'm Jane Radley, a reporter with the *Star Ledger*. Can I buy you a cup of coffee?"

———

Radley carried two coffees to the corner booth where Redford was waiting, and then turned on the small digital recorder she had placed on the table.

"So tell me, Dr. Redford, what exactly is a demon?"

"Do you want the very long answer or the really short one?

"The shorter the better."

"The apocryphal books of the Old Testament say that demons are fallen angels."

"And what's an angel?"

Redford laughed. "Jane, this is like teaching Religion 101. I take it you're not a religious person."

"An atheist from a long line of atheists."

"Well, based on what the Bible and the Koran say, angels are spiritual beings that God uses for various purposes but most frequently as messengers. In fact the English word 'angel' and the Latin 'angelus' are both derived from the Greek 'angelos,' which means 'messenger.'"

"I suppose that's why they need those big wings."

"Yeah, artists like to depict them with wings. But in the Bible angels appear to humans in different forms. You have to realize we are talking about transcendent beings who can operate outside of space-time in different dimensions from us. So we lack the intellectual concepts or words to precisely define or describe them."

"Sounds like quantum mechanics."

"Exactly. And like physicists, a number of early Christian theologians, including Ambrose, Jerome, and Denys, speculated about the unknowable and formulated theories about angels. Denys's work, which is titled 'The Celestial Hierarchy,' is the most comprehensive. It organizes celestial beings into three hierarchies or ranks, with the seraphim and cherubim in the highest and archangels and angels in the lowest—the rank most distant from God and closest to us. Which may be why, according to Denys, archangels and angels have less intelligence and wisdom than celestial beings in the upper hierarchies."

Redford wanted the interview to appear on page one of the *Star Ledger* with a big headline and figured a little spice would help its chances.

"Although Denys doesn't mention it, there are passages in the Bible indicating that angels can be sexually attracted to humans. Genesis 6 tells of 'sons of God' finding human women beautiful and taking them as wives. Early Jewish and Christian scholars believed the 'sons of God' in question were fallen angels. And in 1 Corinthians 11:10, Paul urges women to keep their hair covered because of the angels."

Radley grinned. "This is great stuff. My editor's going to love it. Now tell me what you think. Do you believe in angels?"

The success of Redford's counseling practice depended on his being perceived as both a devout Christian and a hardheaded man of science. So he had to be careful. "Have you ever read 'Peter Pan'?"

"Sure."

"Well, your question reminds me of the scene where Peter warns Wendy that every time someone denies the existence of fairies, a fairy dies."

Radley chuckled amiably and, sensing he wanted to dodge the question, pressed for an answer.

"But, kidding aside, Doc, do you personally believe in angels?"

"Well, Jane, like our modern-day physicists, I realize powerful forces exist that I can't see or understand. So in the face of the prominence given to angels in the Bible and Koran, and the belief in them by thoughtful Christian, Jewish, and Islamic scholars, I'm not prepared to risk killing one off by denying they exist."

—————

Redford went home feeling upbeat because of the publicity, which he expected to generate clientele, book sales, and desperately needed income.

He heated a frozen dinner in the microwave and, to celebrate the day's good fortune, opened a bottle of an herb-fruit wine made by Ellie, the wife of a friend. He had been reluctant to drink it up to that point because Ellie belonged to a new age religion that made sacrificial use of hallucinogenic psilocybin mushrooms, which she grew at home. But he knew her to be sensible, and her wine was the only alcoholic beverage he had on hand.

When he finished dinner and the wine, he inserted the "Exorcist" in his DVD player with a wry smile and sprawled on the sofa where he dozed off half an hour into the film. He slept soundly through the night except for an episode of tachycardia caused by a steamy dream involving a sexual encounter with the woman who saved him from giving a bad answer during the Jackal TV interview.

When he awoke the next morning, the woman was sitting nearby in an armchair.

"Hello, Paul. I'm Bethany."

Despite her commonplace attire—jeans, a white hooded sweatshirt, and sandals—and the slovenly way her long red hair flowed below her shoulders, she was the most beautiful creature he had ever seen. He gasped, and then, remembering Ellie's wine, laughed. He was obviously hallucinating and might as well relax and enjoy it.

"Hello, Bethany. I take it you're the demon I exorcised yesterday."

She frowned. "I prefer 'fallen angel,' which is the term you used earlier."

"Fallen angel it is. So how did you become fallen?"

"I was blamed when a woman corrupted a man who was destined for greatness." She emphasized "destined" for ironic effect.

"I take it you led her into sin."

"He was powerful, devious, and determined to have her at any cost. So I encouraged her to go with the flow and save herself. Since then I've been considered too pragmatic and independent-minded to be of use, which is totally unjust. Any fair-minded person would approve of the outcomes I produce."

"Like getting Cruz to rob the store."

"He wanted to go to a community college but couldn't get a job to earn the tuition. I encouraged him to look for work and even helped with the interviews, but all the offers were minimum wage. A couple more robberies and he'd have enough for the first semester."

"What about the store owners?"

"They all have more money than they need."

"He could have killed someone."

"I would have discouraged that unless it was in self defense."

"Okay I get it. You've got a good heart. And you certainly are very beautiful. Did you appear like this to Hector?"

"A slightly younger version. But I can't take credit for the design. I look like a real woman who lived long ago."

"Let me guess. Her name was 'Bethany.'"

"No, 'Bathsheba.'"

Redford howled. "I get it! The object of King David's lust in the first book of Solomon! The woman who got you into trouble. I love this! I gotta get me some more of that wine!"

"Anyway," she continued, ignoring the outburst, "although I liked Hector, I was bored out of my mind and couldn't believe my luck when you came on the scene."

She got up and sat next to him on the sofa.

"Look, Paul, I think we should work together. We would make a good team. You know a lot about theology and human psychology. I would contribute pragmatism and common sense accumulated over the centuries. No one has enough of them."

"I don't think so, Beth," he said gently.

"How can you say 'no' to this kind of opportunity? Working with me would make you a famous psychologist. Your practice and income would grow. You'd help more people. And what about intellectual curiosity? You're a scholar. The scholarly thing to do would be to see what you can learn from me."

She saw he was still unconvinced, and added, "I know I can learn a lot from you, Paul."

Redford's eyes met hers, which radiated admiration back at him.

"And remember," she concluded, "it wouldn't be a Faustian bargain. You know my name and can send me packing whenever you like."

Redford scratched his head thoughtfully.

"Bethany, I want you to know that I realize you're just a hallucination, and that I'm thinking up all the persuasive arguments you're making. But, for the fun of it, let's say I agreed to take you on as an apprentice on a probationary basis. Would you promise to stay out of my dreams? I don't like being manipulated that way."

She giggled softly. "I would if you insisted, even though I find you very attractive."

"All right then, we'll give it a try," he said, and added with a mischievous smile, "at least until the mushrooms wear off."

His cell phone rang.

"I'll let you take that in privacy," she said and faded from sight.

The call was from his agent.

———

Paul ate breakfast, dressed, and arrived at his office in plenty of time for an eleven thirty a.m. appointment. Bethany had not reappeared, so the wine was apparently out of his system.

The appointment was with a second-year seminarian named Harold Bidwell whom a local bishop had asked him to see. Bidwell had admitted to his superiors that, as alleged in an anonymous letter to the Bishop, he had in the past viewed child pornography on the Internet. But he insisted he was controlling the temptation with prayer and it was no longer a problem.

The Bishop told Redford that Bidwell was a brilliant scholar and an extraordinary public speaker with tremendous potential to inspire believers and spread the faith. He said he did not want to expel him from the seminary unless it was absolutely necessary, and hoped Redford could help him avoid having to do that.

Bidwell arrived without an apology half an hour late for the appointment. He was a tall, impressive-looking young man with a resonant voice and an enormous ego.

Ignoring the fact that Redford was an accredited theologian, Bidwell proceeded to lecture him at great length on a theory formulated by the theologian Augustine of Hippo in the fifth century, which Bidwell distorted to fit his own views.

"And so," he concluded, "although we have been cleansed from original sin, it has left us weakened and with an intense and irrational desire to take physical pleasure from the bodies of our fellow human beings. Augustine's writings attest to how difficult it is to distinguish between unavoidable misconduct caused by the aftereffects of original sin, on the one hand, and the voluntary personal sin for which one is accountable, on the other. Therefore, although we're obliged to try to resist illicit sexual behavior, it's important not to get too down on ourselves when we fail."

Redford was outraged and about to launch a take-no-prisoners-attack on Bidwell's self-serving moral theology when he heard Bethany's voice crystal clear inside his head.

"Don't get sidetracked, Paul. Take him over to the window and ask him to say what comes into his mind."

He was stunned but quickly recovered and walked to the window, which he was surprised to find wide open. He looked out and saw that the schoolyard, four stories down and across the street, was filled with prepubescent children lined up in fire drill formation. He asked Bidwell to join him at the window.

"What do you think when you look at those kids, Harold?"

Bidwell leaned out the window for a better look.

"My very first thoughts were probably the same ones you had."

"Like what?"

"Can I be candid?"

"You have to be if you want my help. I'm bound by professional ethics to keep what you say confidential."

Bidwell smiled and proceeded to describe his perverted fantasies.

Redford felt a powerful urge to push him out the window and say it was suicide, but managed to restrain himself. "No, I'll tell the Bishop the guy's a psycho who should be expelled from the seminary immediately. If he refuses, I'll go to the media, physician-patient confidentiality be damned. It'd cost me patient referrals from the diocese and maybe a license suspension for the ethical violation, but protecting children is more important."

Again he heard Bethany's voice. "I like your thinking, Paul. You're being unselfish and have your priorities right. But the assisted suicide approach has its advantages. Bear in mind that Bidwell will continue to be a threat to innocent children after he's expelled from the seminary. You may someday regret not having done more to stop him."

Collecting all the determination he could muster, Redford took the seminarian by the elbow and led him away from the window.

"Harold, I'm sorry. I just remembered I have another appointment in a few minutes. I wish there was more time but you'll recall we started late. I appreciate your candor. It's given me some ideas to mull over."

He ushered Bidwell out of the office, closed the door, and stood with his back pressed against it for several minutes. It had been a close call, and now he had to decide what to do about his new apprentice, who had just entered the room.

*"The gulls were acting the way they do when hovering over a school of frenzy-feeding bluefish while waiting for scraps of flesh and guts to float to the surface."*

# SONGS OF THE SEA

*I have heard the mermaids singing, each to each.*
*I do not think they will sing to me.*
T.S. Elliot, "The Love Song of J. Alfred Prufrock"

As usual at breakfast time, the Spinnaker Diner was crowded, noisy, and redolent of bacon, eggs, and coffee. Three members of the Seal Isle Police Department, who constituted its entire staff, were enjoying food and conversation at the corner booth that was reserved for them every morning. Captain Percy Clogg, age sixty-one, had headed the Department for as long as anyone could remember. Officer Athena Bickford, twenty-eight and divorced, was taking night courses on criminal justice at the community college and considered herself a career law enforcer. Officer Peter Beal, a chaste twenty-four-year-old, was an ex-seminarian who had interrupted his studies in order to support a widowed sister and her young children. He had been a year from ordination and planned to return to the seminary as soon as his sister could work full-time.

Peter and Athena found one another attractive but knew a divorced police officer would be an unsuitable wife for an Episcopal priest. So they kept their feelings to themselves and their relationship purely collegial—although she was somewhat less committed to this state of affairs than he was.

The Captain's cell phone rang with the tone he assigned to calls forwarded from the station house. He hurriedly swallowed a mouthful of omelet.

"Police Department, Clogg speaking." After listening for several minutes, he said, "Sure, Jens, I'll do that. We'll tell him. The crew and I are in the middle of breakfast, but as soon as we're done, I'll send Peter over to the Cove. You're welcome, Jens. Bye."

Athena smiled. "Let me guess. Some guy rented the Conway house, and Jens wants you to warn him about the big squid."

"You got it," said Clogg resignedly. He took a sip of coffee and turned to Peter.

"You recall the death of a guy named Conroy a couple of years ago over at Lobster Cove?"

"Yeah. I was at the seminary, but my sister told me about it. He owned the house there."

"Right. He used it on weekends as a love nest. Seemed like a different woman every time. A regular Don Juan."

"Or Marquis De Sade, for all we know," Athena added.

"Then this one weekend he comes up alone, and doesn't show up at his office the following Monday. Athena and I went out to the house and didn't find anything odd except for an overturned beach chair and some churned-up sand just above the high tide line. His car was in the driveway, and his wallet and keys were in the house. Couple of days later a fisherman found his body wedged between some rocks a quarter mile offshore. The autopsy showed death by loss of blood and shock, not drowning. All of his internal organs had been removed through a hole chewed in his abdomen while he was still alive."

"Eels?" Peter asked with a grimace.

"No. The kinds we have around here don't attack the living. Anyway, this all rang a bell with Jens Nilsson at the tackle shop. He did some computer research on people who have gone missing off the Maine coast, and found reports that some of the recovered bodies had been disemboweled. Jens is convinced Conroy and the others were snatched and sucked dry by a Kraken."

"Kraken?"

"It's a legendary Scandinavian sea monster with a taste for human innards. I never heard of it either. Jens made such a fuss I looked it up on Wikipedia."

"Athena mentioned a squid."

"Wikipedia says mariners' myths always have a basis in reality. Sailors once believed in sea serpents because so many real things look like them—porpoises swimming one behind the other, large masses of floating kelp half awash. Columbus wrote in a logbook during his second voyage that he saw mermaids, which were probably manatees. In the case of the Kraken, scholars attribute the legend to sightings of giant squids by Vikings and other early seafarers."

"So," Athena added with a grin, "Scotland has the Loch Ness monster and Seal Isle has a giant gut-sucking squid, which, unfortunately, isn't as good for tourism."

Peter laughed. "You know there's a Biblical side to sea monsters. At the time the Book of Genesis was written, there was an ancient tale about Yahweh having to defeat a sea dragon in order to create the Cosmos. Since it wasn't included in the biblical account of Creation, it looks like there were monster skeptics even back then."

Athena smirked. "Thanks for the sermon, Reverend, but you should give theology a rest when you're on duty. The Township isn't paying you to save souls."

"Right as usual, Officer Bickford," Peter said good-naturedly. "More to the point, a Kraken supposedly looks like a giant squid, and none of those has ever been sighted in our waters, as far as I know."

"That doesn't mean a thing," Athena said ominously with a twinkle in her eyes. "Remember, all the victims were alone. And though I didn't see

anything when I scuba dived around the Cove looking for Conroy, I felt I was being watched the whole
time."

The Captain laughed. "After listening to Jens,
you can't help being a little spooked."

"What do you think really happened to Conroy,
Cap?" Peter asked.

"No idea. The sea's full of things that can kill
you—rip tides, rogue waves, poisonous jellyfish,
sharks, orcas. Or Conroy could've been murdered
and disemboweled on shore and had his body
dumped in the sea afterward, though that seems unlikely. His family and friends knew of no enemies,
and there were no signs of a mutilating madman being on the loose. Anyway, when we're done here you
need to drive out to the Cove. Jens already warned
the renter but said the guy's a know-it-all and thought
it was funny."

"He'll laugh at me too."

"Not if you leave out the Kraken nonsense and
stick to the facts. Just tell him about Conroy and
suggest he be careful and keep his eyes open when
he's near the water. Jens said his name is 'Harris.'"

———

As Peter left the Diner for Lobster Cove,
Professor of Oceanography Martin Harris was trudg-
ing across the sand, weighted down by a surfcasting
pole, tackle box, cooler, and beach chair. He was

heading toward the stone jetty bisecting the Cove, which seemed a good place from which to fish.

Martin was taking a solitary vacation during spring break so he could think through a knotty personal problem. Last month the college president unexpectedly announced his retirement, and Martin was chosen to succeed him next term. This meant that over the next few months he had to end a secret affair with Heather, his teaching assistant. He knew if he did not handle it right, the little bitch, as he now thought of her, would ruin him. She had lately become very clingy and would be with him now had she not committed to a Windjammer cruise with a girlfriend. Martin sighed, peered out onto the choppy sea, and wondered whether Windjammer cruises were at all dangerous. He had seriously considered looking for an ex-con to take the cruise and arrange a shipboard accident. But then he remembered how people were sometimes arrested by undercover cops posing as hit men. So if there were dirty work to be done, he would have to do it himself. But he had resolved not to think about any of this unpleasantness today. He had a whole week to do that, and, for now, he was going to relax and enjoy the ocean. Although it was a gloomy day, the Cove was sternly beautiful, and he had it all to himself.

Martin's attention was caught by a flock of gulls circling low and squawking excitedly over a large object in the shallow surf a few hundred feet to his right. The gulls were acting the way they do when hovering over a school of frenzy-feeding bluefish while waiting for scraps of flesh and guts to float to the surface. He grinned, remembering the crazy old Swede babbling about a local sea monster. Seeing the situation's potential as an amusing cocktail party story, he hurriedly shed his gear and jogged toward the gulls.

When he was halfway to the object, his heart jumped. Partially in the water lay the body of a naked woman wrapped in kelp.

"Heather," he exclaimed hopefully, but when he got closer he saw it was not she.

The body was that of a beautiful woman with long blonde hair, small breasts, a narrow waist, and extremely white skin. She reminded Martin of Botticelli's painting "The Birth of Venus."

He knelt in the water and placed a hand on the side of her throat to feel for a pulse and, ever the multitasker, he used his other hand to caress one of her breasts. Suddenly her eyes snapped open, and she smiled at him, fondly, as though he were a lover she had been expecting. Martin quickly recovered from his surprise, withdrew his hands, and smiled back, entranced by her exotic beauty, penetrating black eyes, wide mouth, and the silvery flecks that decorated her skin. She looked deeply into his eyes and began to hum a melody in a strange musical mode that conjured up the roar of the wind and the surging of waves, and transported Martin far out onto the ocean. He loved sea birds and now he was one of them, a large Shearwater gliding effortlessly over the waves for miles and miles. He had never been so happy and felt so free. He wanted it to go on forever.

The song stopped, and Martin found himself lying in the shallows with his limbs numb and the woman's hand around his wrist. He felt her grip to be exceptionally strong and saw that her fingers were webbed. Her mouth had shed its gentle, coquettish smile and become a lamprey's mouth, round and full of small serrated teeth. With a series of powerful un-dulating thrusts she shook off the kelp and began to slide into the bay, while Martin, struggling in vain to pull free, screamed in terror.

---

Two hours later Captain Clogg phoned the tackle shop from the house at Lobster Cove.

"Jens, I've got a problem. Harris's car is in the driveway, but he's not in the house or on the beach. We found a sandal near a large clump of seaweed and a lot of churned-up sand. It looks like he was dragged into the water. Yeah, like with Conroy. Now I'm not jumping to any conclusions, but suppose, for the sake of argument, it's a Kraken or some other rare sea critter that's snatching these guys. What would it take to catch and kill it?"

Jens gave an angry response, and the Captain said soothingly, "Okay, okay. I know you're not a monster expert, and what works against one won't work against all. Suppose you just tell me how to kill a Kraken."

He listened intently to Jens's lengthy reply and then summed it up.

"You're saying he waits for the Kraken alone without a weapon, and when it attacks, he pulls it out of the water onto the beach with his bare hands. Shit, Jens, even if I believed that would work, how the hell would I find a 'hero with a pure heart' to do it?"

Jens made a suggestion, and the Captain chuckled, thanked him, and hung up.

He removed his cap and rubbed the top of his head as he searched his memory.

*"Hero with a pure heart," where have I heard that before? Got it! Sir Galahad, the only one of King Arthur's knights who got to see the Holy Grail. He had the strength of ten because his heart was pure.*

Being able to recall something from his early youth pleased him, but his mind quickly returned to the problem at hand. He thought about the media army that would soon invade Seal Isle and how incompetent they would make him look. His investigation of the Conroy case had been perfunctory, because he had assumed that unusual natural causes that wouldn't be repeated were at play. But that seemed ridiculous now that a second man had disappeared the same way from the same beach. The only thing that would save his reputation and job would be to solve the Harris case and do it quickly. No possibility, no matter how remote, could be ignored.

He went out the back door and walked to where Peter was photographing the crime scene.

"Hey, Peter, we need to talk."

———

As it turned out, Clogg need not have worried about the media. Once they got wind of Jens Kraken theory, it became the focal point of their coverage. A typical headline reporting the finding of Harris's body read: "Professor of Oceanography Eviscerated by Mysterious Sea Creature."

And better yet, a flattering video clip of Clogg had appeared on national television. It had a pretty cable newswoman asking the Captain whether he believed in sea monsters, and him answering, with a sly country boy smile, "Katie, honey, I'm sure you can 'preciate why I can't share the details of an ongoin' investigation. But I will say we've thrown out a net that's plenty wide enough to catch any Kraken that may be lurkin' out there."

The last of the out-of-town reporters had finally left, and Clogg planned to drive to the Cove after lunch and end Peter's three-week stakeout. Jens had recommended at least three weeks so the Kraken would have time to digest Harris's innards and become hungry again.

———

It was a foggy day at Lobster Cove with rain expected in the late afternoon. Out on the beach, Peter lay on a chaise lounge reading a novel Athena had lent him. It was about an idealistic and high-principled husband and his resourceful and courageous wife who struggle against a never-ending stream of calamities. Reading while on stakeout was okay, Jens said, because the water around a submerged Kraken omitted such a horrible odor that you always smelled one before you saw it. And Jens had no objection to Peter wearing his service pistol, provided he left it behind when he went to fight the Kraken *mano y mano*. This was all nonsense to Peter, but it was what the Captain wanted and happened to be the most pleasant assignment he had ever had.

He felt hungry and checked his watch. Fifteen more minutes and he would head back to the beach house where Athena would be meeting him with lunch from the Diner. The food she brought was always delicious and was paid for by the Department because of the stakeout.

Knowing Athena would want to discuss the novel over lunch, he dutifully opened it and resumed reading. He had covered only half a page when his attention was caught by the cries of gulls circling something in the surf.

He sniffed the air and smiled. "No stench, no Kraken," he said to himself, and headed toward the object, walking at first and then running when he saw it was a body. It was that of a slender woman, lying half out of the water with arms by her sides and long blonde hair spread out on the damp sand. Her upper torso was naked and the lower, wrapped in kelp.

*Lord, she's exquisite. Like a Renaissance painting*, he thought.

He averted his eyes from her bare breasts, squatted in the water, and felt her throat for a pulse. Now up close, he saw that her skin was covered with silvery flecks and her mouth was unusually wide.

He was not finding a heartbeat, so, when she opened her eyes and smiled, he was startled and toppled backward to a sitting position in the shallow water.

"You're alive! Are you okay?" he asked, returning her smile.

Her answer was to look deeply into his eyes and begin vocalizing in a strange musical mode that made him think of Gregorian chant, although it was nothing like it. He loved church music and tried to mentally visualize the notes she was making. Suddenly he found himself clothed in gorgeous priestly vestments and giving a sermon from the pulpit of a vast cathedral filled with worshippers who were spellbound by his eloquence.

He was dimly aware that he was daydreaming and wanted to pull out of it. Numbness in his arms and legs prevented him from moving, but he found he could summon his voice and began to sing an eighteenth century Protestant hymn.

"O God our help in ages past, our hope in years to come. Our shelter from the stormy blast, and our eternal home."

He felt his strength returning as he sang.

Looking amused, the creature changed to a throbbing, sensual vocalization and pulled away some of the kelp covering her lower body. This revealed more nakedness, including a pair of graceful thighs that began to spread as she bent her knees.

Peter was overcome by a potent lust that made copulating with her a dire necessity. With his heart racing, he stopped singing and crawled to her side. But just as she reached out to guide him onto her, he was jolted to his senses by a powerful impact that hurled him back up onto the beach. He had been hit by a five-foot wall of water, the first in a train of swells to arrive at the Cove from a storm raging thousands of miles away off the coast of Africa.

He scrambled to his feet, grabbed one of the woman's arms, and pulled her onto the sand with the help of another breaking wave. The remaining kelp fell away, and he saw to his horror that her feet were fused at the heels and pointed sideways form-ing a caudal fin.

"You're not human—you're a monster," he shout-ed, nauseated by the thought of what had almost happened.

She looked terrified and began omitting a pite-ous keening sound. Peter drew his pistol and tried to aim it between her eyes but, affected by her lament, could not keep the sight on target. He changed to a two-handed grip, which steadied his aim, but then could not bring himself to pull the trigger. Inhuman though she might be, she was too beautiful a crea-ture to destroy. And, after all, he was there to kill a Kraken, not a sea siren—maybe the last one left on Earth. Sure she was a seductress, but that did not warrant a death sentence. He recalled that Jesus be-friended Mary Magdalene, who had been possessed by seven demons and had likely done some shame-ful things. No, he would spare her, put her back in the sea.

He lifted the creature from the sand and carried her toward the jetty. Her body was cool, light, and motionless in his arms, and her face serene. She be-gan to hum, softly and tenderly. The hungry gulls were back now, circling and crying overhead. Peter felt his attraction to her growing with every step he took. He climbed onto the jetty and gingerly made his way over the rocks to its tip, where he stood holding her in his arms while trying to think of a way he could keep her. But he realized it could not be done. He would put her back and let her come to him again, if she chose. He would return that night after dark and bring her food.

As though reading his mind, she turned her face to him, smiled, and gently draped an arm over his shoulder. Her touch thrilled him. At that moment he loved her unconditionally.

He stepped to the end of the jetty, slowly went down to his knees, kissed her forehead, and let her fall a short distance to the sea, not realizing she had a tight grip on his collar. This pulled him off balance and toppled him into the bay after her. He popped to the surface smiling at her playfulness, and treaded water while waiting for her to appear. Instead, she wrapped her arms tightly around his hips, fastened her lamprey mouth onto his abdomen, and began to chew through his clothing.

"Stop, stop!" he screamed, managing to hold her head inches away from his body by pushing with all his might. She responded with a powerful undulating thrust that drove him deep under the water. He struggled valiantly to break free, but the creature was strong and they were now entirely in her element. In less than a minute the oxygen in his lungs was expended by the exertion, and, yielding to the primal urge to inhale, he aspirated salt water and lost consciousness. Happily free of restraint, the creature began to leisurely chew into his intestines, while, at the surface, the gulls picked bits of his flesh off of the blood-tinted sea.

At that moment, Athena Bickford, who had been waiting for Peter at the house, began to walk down the beach to meet him.

*Rewind and replay with Peter's Sermon to the sea creature added.*

He climbed onto the jetty and gingerly made his way over the rocks to its tip, where he stood holding her in his arms while trying to think of a way he could keep her. But he realized it could not be done. He would put her back and let her come to him again, if she chose. He would return that night after dark and bring her food. And he would do his utmost to save her soul, beginning now with a sermon flowing directly from his heart.

"Beautiful creature, I don't know whether you can understand me or even what you are. But I'm certain the same God made us both, as he did every living thing that inhabits this planet or any other. And I truly believe that, human being or not, you have an immortal soul just as I do. A man named Henry Beston wrote a beautiful book about a year he spent observing nature and wildlife near the sea. I've read it so many times that I know parts by heart, although I never expected to use them in my ministry, except maybe to comfort someone who had lost a pet. The part I like best, that really rings true to me, is his observation that humankind errs when it patronizes animals and measures them against itself. 'In a world older than ours they move finished and complete, gifted with extensions of the senses we have lost or never attained, living by voices we shall never hear. They are not brethren, they are not underlings: they are other nations caught with ourselves in the net of life and time.'"

Peter, who loved animals, was always deeply moved by these words. He squeezed her gently, and there were tears in his eyes.

"You have my promise. I'll bring you food so you won't have to kill to survive. I'll encourage you to use your amazing gift of song to give comfort. And I'll protect you."

She had been watching him intently throughout the sermon, and now she smiled and gently draped an arm over his shoulder. He was sure she understood him, if not the words at least the sentiment behind them. She would kill no more.

He stepped to the end of the jetty, slowly went down to his knees, kissed her forehead, and let her fall a short distance to the sea, not realizing she had a tight grip on his collar. This pulled him off balance and toppled him into the bay after her. He popped to the surface smiling at her playfulness, and treaded water while waiting for her to appear. Instead, she wrapped her arms tightly around his hips, fastened her lamprey mouth onto his abdomen, and began to chew through his clothing.

"Stop, stop!" he screamed, managing to hold her head inches away from his body by pushing with all his might. She responded with a powerful undulating thrust that drove him deep under the water. He struggled valiantly to break free, but the creature was strong and they were now entirely in her element.

Out of oxygen, he was on the verge of aspirating sea water when he heard a muffled thump, felt her release him, and glimpsed her darting toward deeper water trailing blood. He pushed to the surface gasping for air, and, when he had blinked his eyes clear, saw grim-faced policewoman Athena Bickford standing at the edge of the jetty, pistol in hand, like an avenging angel. Like *his* avenging angel.

*"And they fly away."*

# A VERY BAD DAY AT THE MOVIES

It was a Saturday during the year 1947 in Astoria, New York. The Cameo Theatre's marquee announced a matinee that started at noon and consisted of ten cartoons, a cliffhanger serial, a comedy short, and a cowboy feature—all for an admission price of ten cents for kids and twenty-five for adults.

The Cameo needed to offer bargain-priced kiddy matinees on weekends, as well as free dishes and other gifts on weekdays, because it was small and dumpy, and showed films that were years past first run. The huge theatre palaces that showed new releases, like the gigantic, ornate Loew's only a block away on Steinway Street, did not provide such incentives.

Two out-of-breath boys arrived at the Cameo's ticket window a minute before showtime. Billy and Tommy were eight-year-old classmates who lived in the same five-story brick apartment building on

111

Thirty-Eighth Street, a block from the Cameo. After buying their tickets, they regretfully bypassed the refreshment stand because it was mobbed, and dashed into the theatre hoping to find decent seats.

Inside, chaos reigned. The auditorium was filled with noisy, hyperactive kids being managed by four uniformed ushers who tried to herd them into seats and stop them from running up and down the aisles. Tranquility existed only in the small section in the back reserved for adults who were accompanying children.

The Boys spotted and took two undesirable seats together at the end of the third row. Almost immediately the house lights dimmed and the first cartoon, a Tom and Jerry, began. As was customary, this evoked a loud cheer, and then all conversation ceased. The only sounds uttered during the remainder of the program were movie-induced laughter, screams of terror, and the like. In pre-television America, the movies offered children a unique experience that commanded rapt attention.

The cliffhanger serial that followed the cartoons was "Nyoka the Jungle Girl," a Republic Pictures production inspired by an Edgar Rice Burroughs novel.

The basic plot was simple. A beautiful and serious-minded young woman named Nyoka lived in the jungle with her father, a doctor who treated the natives. The local tribe had lots of diamonds, and Nyoka wanted to take some of them back to civilization where she would sell them and use the proceeds to have a hospital built for the natives.

She was assisted by Stanton, a handsome bush pilot replete with jodhpurs and riding boots, by Stanton's slightly goofy sidekick, Curly, and by Kimbu, a native boy who was about Billy and Tommy's age. Opposing them were a band of white crooks and members of an evil tribe, who, like all the other natives in the serial, were played by white actors with bronze-tinted skin and bushy wigs of kinky black hair. Characters were killed off in every episode but the killing was always painless, blood-less, and over quickly.

Billy and Tommy adored Nyoka. In the role, Frances Gifford projected intelligence, kindness, courage, and purity. The last virtue resonated strongly with the Boys, who were Catholic and had been taught by the nuns to venerate and pray to the Blessed Virgin.

But it was not only Nyoka's good looks and ster-ling character that captured their hearts. She was also an amazing athlete who flew through the jungle from vine to vine, rode an elephant, and dove into la-goons from high cliffs. This was obviously why her otherwise demure outfit, with its high neckline, long sleeves, and fashionably padded shoulders, needed to have an extremely short skirt.

As befitting a cliffhanger serial, every episode ended with Nyoka, Stanton, or Curly facing some form of exotic doom at the hands of the villains. The

Boys loved it when Kimbu, with whom they identi-fied, helped save Nyoka. They treasured the scene where he was injured and she knelt over him and administered first aid.

It was obvious to the Boys that Kimbu was Nyoka's favorite. Her relationship with Stanton was a purely pragmatic one. She needed him to fly her and the diamonds to civilization. True, she always deferred to him despite being far more capable in the jungle than he. And occasionally, to the Boys' annoyance, she allowed him to lead her by the el-bow. But this was, after all, to be expected of a lady.

The serial had been going on for fourteen weeks, and this Saturday's would be the final installment. As usual, the episode began where the previous one had ended:

*Nyoka, looking terrified, is tied to a stake across from a giant crossbow that will hurl a spear into her chest when a fire burns through a restraining cord. The crooks and the evil natives gleefully look on. Curly arrives and saves Nyoka by swinging on a vine and knocking over the stake she is tied to just as the spear is launched. Meanwhile, Kimbu and Stanton, whose bloodless bullet wound from the prior episode Kimbu has just treated and ban-daged, recruit some good natives and go in search of Nyoka. They arrive just in time to save her and Curly from being burned at the stake by the evil natives, whose leader they kill.*

*The crooks now have the diamonds and are on their way to the plane. But Nyoka, Stanton, Kimbu, Curly, and the good natives head them off. A gunfight ensues during which all the crooks, except Lattimer, their leader, are killed. Lattimer takes off in Stanton's plane with Stanton clinging to a wheel, but does not get far. Stanton climbs into the cockpit and, while struggling with Lattimer, tilts the plane so that the villain falls out the door to his presumably painless and bloodless death.*

*The final scene opens with Nyoka, Stanton, Curly, Kimbu, and a contingent of good natives standing alongside the plane. Nyoka reminds the natives that she will be using the diamonds for their benefit and promises Kimbu she will return. Then Stanton climbs into the pilot seat, Nyoka takes the one next to him, Curly climbs into the back, and they fly away.*

Billy and Tommy were stunned. Nyoka should have taken Kimbu with her. There was room for him in back with Curly. She said she would return, but would she? Her father had been killed off in an earlier episode, and Stanton might well propose marriage. She could use the money from the diamonds to hire people to build and run the hospital without herself returning to the jungle. Would she come back just for Kimbu's sake? Her lack of warmth when they parted was worrisome. Considering all that she and Kimbu had been through together and the help he had given her, why didn't she kiss him or at least give him a hug?

The Boys sat dully through the Laurel and Hardy short and Roy Rogers cowboy feature without finding any joy in them. Afterward, neither felt like joining the swarm of kids engaged in marble-shooting and stickball out in the sunshine on Thirty-Eighth Street. Instead, they fetched Tommy's basketball and, for half an hour, played twenty-one by themselves in a gloomy alley, using the space between the lower two rungs of a fire escape ladder as a basket. They spoke little and neither mentioned the serial.

Fortunately, with the resilience of youth, the Boys were able to shake off bruised feelings as easily as they could ignore a scraped knee during a ball game. So when they returned to the Cameo a week later, they were in high spirits and eagerly looking forward to the first episode of "The Green Hornet."

But although the prior week's disappointment was forgotten, Nyoka herself never left them. She remained tucked away deep in their subconscious minds from where, years later, she would serve as the gold standard by which they measured the unsuspecting women they met at parties and singles dances.

*"The Eye of Liberty" Curfew Enforcement Satellite.*

# MISMANAGED LOVE

I t was a balmy evening in June 2077. Brad E-1432 was the only passenger in an electric taxi heading uptown on Park Avenue in Manhattan.

Both he and the driver were wearing Government-issue survival suits consisting of a jumpsuit, combat boots, gloves, and plastic globe helmet. Their names and bar codes were etched on the helmets just below mouth level.

Brad had seen no one on the streets since the cab picked him up, and he was looking for lights or other signs of occupancy in the buildings they passed. He recalled that a million and a half people once lived in the city, and he imagined crowds of them walking the streets without survival suits, their bare faces exposed to one another.

*A great time to be living*, he thought. Nostalgia was not normally Brad's thing, but this was a special day in his life.

The driver interrupted his reverie. "Hey, officer, I never carry a Mountie before." A patch on Brad's navy blue jumpsuit read "Department of Homeland Security Mounted Police."

"Well, don't think that entitles you to speed or run lights," Brad said with mock severity.

The driver laughed. "But why you takin' a cab? Your scooter broke?"

"No. I'm off-duty. On my way to meet the mother of my child-to-be."

"Repro duty! Congratulations, man. First time?"

"Yep."

"Mind my askin' how old you are?"

"Twenty-six."

"Whoa! Must be a woman shortage. I was eighteen when I had my first woman and have had four more since."

"Five different women?

"Yep."

"Well, I'll want the same one every time. The Repro Division says you can do this if both partners agree."

"Don't believe everything you hear, man. I wanted that too."

"Maybe the women...maybe the women wanted variety."

"Ha! You wouldn't say that if you saw me naked. But, hey, you're finally gettin' your shot, so I better dodge the potholes so we don't damage your equipment."

The cab dropped Brad at a handsome residential hotel adjacent to Central Park. There being no doorman, he showed himself into the elegant lobby and looked around. There were fresh flowers on the reception desk with a sign reading "Welcome Carla B-9094 and Brad E-1432," but there was no one behind the desk or anywhere else in sight. A sign near the elevator said it was out of service, so he walked up eight floors.

The stairwell and eighth floor corridor were empty and quiet. The door to Suite 82 led into a standard air shower stall. Brad closed the door, flipped the switch, and stood still while the shower did its work. A recording prompted him to bend his right leg to expose the bottom of his boot to the air spray and then to do the same with his left. When the shower stopped and the suction vacuum ran its course, he opened the inner door and stepped into the apartment. No sign of Carla, but this was not surprising since he was thirty minutes early.

He removed his helmet and explored the apartment. It consisted of a small kitchen, a combination living room-dining room, a balcony overlooking Central Park, a bedroom with king size bed, and a bathroom containing a large sunken tub surrounded by unlit candles.

On the kitchen counter he found two half-gallon jugs of water and six RTEs—ready-to-eat vegetarian meals, each labeled with either his name or Carla's. Two of the meals were in blue packaging, two in yellow, and two in green, designating dinner, breakfast and lunch.

There was also a letter from Harvey J-5643, Secretary of Health and Human Services, saying they would be picked up the next afternoon and taken to a house on the New Jersey shore for a one-week honeymoon.

Brad walked back to the living room, plopped on the sofa, and switched on the TV. He surfed the channels and was happy to see that the Reproduction Channel was available. It had been unblocked on his home set the day he received email notification of the repro assignment. The Channel offered clinical lectures on reproduction, instruction on the art of lovemaking, and romantic scenes from old movies that he had never heard of, which he enjoyed and watched repeatedly. He wanted to be a sensitive and effective lover for Carla and hoped she felt the same way about him.

He surfed past the Repro Channel, feeling it would be indelicate to have it on when Carla walked in, and settled on the History Channel, which was showing a documentary about the chaos that ensued when the deadly pathogen known as the "Armageddon Bug" was unleashed against America and spread worldwide.

Then hearing the air shower start up, he switched off the TV, and stood facing the door expectantly.

All he knew about Carla was her name. The Government said it was better if the repro couple handled their own introductions and that photos were not furnished because they could be misleading. The interior shower door opened and Carla stepped into the apartment. She was wearing a white jump-suit, which indicated she worked in the medical field.

"Hello, Carla. I'm Brad."

"Yes, how do you do, Brad." Her helmet's amplification system made her voice sound emotionless and metallic. His view of her face through the tinted UV coating on the helmet was the equivalent of low resolution video. And because survival suits were loose fitting he had no idea of her figure, although it was safe to assume she was slender like everyone else living on RTEs.

Brad, who had never been in the presence of a woman whose face was exposed, was eager for Carla to remove her helmet. She could do this because couples in repro were exempted from the requirement that complete survival suits be worn whenever in the presence of others.

"So are you going to take off your helmet and stay a while?" he asked with a smile.

"Oh sure," she said, and hurriedly removed it.

They stood motionless and stared intently at one another for a full half a minute, during which each of these ordinary looking young people privately pronounced the other beautiful. Because face-to-face encounters between the sexes were precluded by the survival suit law, repro sessions were usually intense Adam-meets-Eve experiences.

Glancing at Brad's navy blue jumpsuit, Carla nervously tossed a conversational gambit.

"So you work for Homeland Security?"

"Yeah, I'm in the Mounted Police. A Mountie," he said, pointing to the patch on his arm and feeling silly as he did it.

"Does that white outfit mean you're a doctor?"

"No. A pharmacist. I help plan and supervise the inclusion of additives in MREs, you know, vitamins, special nutritional supplements, medication."

He nodded.

"But what I really need to tell you, Brad, is that I'm very sorry, but I'm not going to repro. I'm going to report my decision now and leave."

Brad was stunned. "Why? We've been assigned to each other. Don't you like me?"

"No, that's not it! I don't even know you. And you look fine. It's the repro program that I don't like. If we lived under the old ways I would definitely want to marry and become a mother, but not like this."

"Like this?"

"You've got to compare it to the way people lived before the Bug. The way it's described in the novels."

"It's illegal to read that stuff."

"No, it isn't," she snapped. "Only reprinting or copying them because that would use scarce national resources. As a cop you should know that."

He blushed and stammered, "I'm sorry. I didn't mean…."

She regretted having embarrassed him.

"It's okay. Most people think novels are illegal because they are so hard to come by. And I know you Mounties have more important things to worry about than whether people are Xeroxing Jane Austin. Anyway, please understand my decision has nothing to do with you."

"Then why didn't you report it right away and not wait until you saw me?"

"I did, but they insisted that I meet you before making a final decision. I guess they figured I was nervous and might change my mind."

Agitated and needing to vent, Brad walked across the room and back.

"I don't like to say this, Carla, but I don't understand how you can be so damn self-centered and unpatriotic. If every woman refused repro we would die out."

She struggled to restrain a smile. "That's true, but the fact is that they don't and if it came to that I might reconsider. But maybe if enough of us say 'no' to repro, the Government will improve the system. Like in that Greek play, 'Lysistrata,' where the women deny the men sex until they end a stupid war."

"Well, I don't know anything about Greek plays, but I think repro works just fine."

"So you approve of couples having to part as soon as there's pregnancy and of mothers having to surrender their newborns?"

"The parents are needed back at work and have to separate to minimize the risk of infection. And they get unlimited visitation with the child."

"Yeah, but visitation ends when the kid reaches twelve and then the three of them have to be put on antidepressants while they adjust. Don't fool yourself, Brad. The Government could improve things if it wanted to."

Resigned to his fate, Brad asked, "So what's going to happen now?"

"I'll email my decision from here and return to my apartment. I'll be questioned and possibly demoted, but they'll leave me alone after that. Boycotting repro isn't a crime, at least not yet."

"What about me?" he asked.

"You'll be assigned another partner, and in the meantime they'll put you back on Nilid."

"Nilid?"

"The sex-urge suppressant."

"They put that in my food?"

Carla bit her tongue. She had just disclosed classified medical information, and to a cop no less. She realized acting guilty was the worst thing she could do and decided to put Brad on the defensive.

"Sure. I thought you would know about it, being in law enforcement and all. Every sexually mature adult who's not in repro gets Nilid. That's why we have no sex crimes. But of course this is closely held information, not meant for the general public and apparently not for all policemen either."

"Do they add other things, besides vitamins and antibiotics and things like that?"

"Sedatives sometimes to help you get a good night's sleep if you've been showing signs of stress, and mild intoxicants to help you enjoy holidays. But, as the Government says, it's for our own good. Living alone is difficult for most people so they help us cope. That's why they tint our helmets and have the helmet amp systems distort our voices. It prevents emotional involvement at the workplace."

"No, the helmet tinting is for UV ray blocking."

"Yes, but it's darker than it has to be. It's hard to become attached to someone whose face is barely visible and whose voice sounds like everyone else's. Makes it easier for us to spend most of our lives in virtual solitary confinement, which the Government says we have to do as long as the Bug's around."

Brad mulled it over. He sensed she was worried and wanted to help.

"Thanks for telling me about this, Carla. I'll keep everything you said to myself. You have my word."

She was relieved and smiled at him gratefully.

"Now will you do one small favor for me?" he asked. "Stay just a little while longer, to talk, that's all. This is my first time face-to-face with a woman, and it must be the same for you with men."

Her eyes were sympathetic, but she shook her head.

"Have you ever seen the Ocean?" he asked.

"No."

"Neither have I. They've got a week's vacation at the seashore planned for us starting tomorrow. Suppose we take it? There'd be no repro, only, uh, uh...."

"Companionship?"

"Yeah, companionship," he agreed, although he was not sure what the word meant. "We could erect some kind of a 'Wall of Jericho' between us on the bed, like in that movie."

"It Happened One Night."

Brad faked a shocked expression. "Wait a second. Don't tell me that Carla the conscientious objector has been watching the Repro channel," he said in mock outrage

"Not the sex demos, just the old romantic movies," she said giggling. "I swear it."

He laughed. "Well, how about it then? A week of companionship at the seashore?"

She slowly shook her head. "I'm really sorry, Brad. I just don't want to make this harder than it already is. But trust me. The next woman they send will be overjoyed she is paired with you. You really are a very nice guy and not bad looking either."

She sent her email, they solemnly shook hands, and she left. Brad watched sadly from the balcony as she walked away from the hotel and out of his life.

———

Back at his apartment, Brad received email notification that he would start a new repro assignment
in two weeks and should return to work until then.
His repro partner was to be Kelli R-7729.

Because of the new assignment, Brad's meals
continued to be Nilid-free, and he soon started having erotic dreams involving Carla, which made him
feel like he was cheating on Kelli even though he
had never met her. So he began volunteering for
overtime shifts in the hope that fatigue would lead
to dreamless sleep.

The principal function of Homeland Security
Mounties was to arrest "roamers"—people who
leave their dwellings without authorization. All citizens had micro transponders implanted on their
skulls so their whereabouts could be tracked by a
geo-stationary satellite called "The Eye of Liberty."
Data from the Eye was transmitted to Homeland
Security Department computers that checked it
against a database containing the times each citizen
was authorized to leave his or her home for work
or other purposes. When roamers were detected,
Mounties from the nearest precinct were dispatched
to take them into custody, using tranquilizer darts if
necessary.

It was the day before Brad's scheduled rendez-
vous with Kelli, and he was on the late night shift
patrolling lower Manhattan on his scooter. His radio
suddenly crackled an order to back up a wounded

Mountie who had happened upon citizens burglarizing the west side RTE warehouse.

*Why would anyone steal food that was distributed free?* he wondered. The government occasionally reported inventory shortfalls at the warehouses but always attributed them to bookkeeping errors.

Galvanized by the situation, he raced to the warehouse with his siren wailing. There he found a Mountie, hands and face covered with blood, sitting on the ground near a scooter with a shredded front tire. He waved Brad away.

"Don't worry about me. There're two of them and they went down Ninth. Keep your distance 'til backup comes. They've got a shotgun."

Brad sped off in pursuit and, five blocks down, spotted two men walking at a fast pace on the sidewalk to his right. They saw him and turned the corner at Forty-Seventh Street. Realizing he would have to follow them on foot if they went into one of the narrow alleys off Forty-Seventh, he stopped, removed his tranquilizer rifle from its scabbard, and slung it crossways over his back. Resuming pursuit, he rounded the corner at full throttle and found the men waiting for him in the middle of the street. In a single instant, he saw a flash, heard a loud blast, felt stinging in his legs and abdomen, and realized he was flying off the scooter.

Brad awoke on a stretcher in a hospital emergency room. The attending doctor said the good news was he had sustained only a mild concussion and superficial wounds. The bad was he would be kept at the hospital in isolation for the full duration of the Armageddon Bug's incubation period because his helmet had shattered and he had been exposed to unfiltered air. Reacting to the terror in Brad's eyes, the doctor quickly added that infection was unlikely because emergency responders had covered his face with a breathing mask within minutes of the crash.

Two things of note happened during Brad's confinement: his repro assignment with Kelli was cancelled and he was awarded the Presidential Medal for Bravery. He learned about the medal on his second day in the hospital while eating dinner. The intercom clicked and his nurse said, "Brad, turn your TV to Channel 2. Your picture was just on. The President said you and the other wounded Mountie are going to get medals for risking your lives to protect the food supply."

He switched to Channel 2, and there was President George P-0001 sitting behind his desk in the Oval Office concluding a speech. He was dressed in a modest gray jumpsuit, and his helmet was beside him on the desk.

"Our war against extinction is now entering a new and even more dangerous phase in which we are pitted against an organization of anarchistic deviants who want to upset the delicate equilibrium that is critical to our survival. Their potential to wreak havoc is very great. They are ruthless and well armed and have a sophisticated technical capability that enables them to avoid detection by the Eye of Liberty System. So I depend on every American to take this threat seriously, to be vigilant, and to report any suspicious behavior or remarks by fellow citizens. I know that together as a Nation we will overcome this threat and mercilessly grind these deviants into the dust. God bless America."

Brad liked the President because he seemed to be a regular guy who was just trying to do his job like everyone else. His grandfather, Thomas Jefferson Hopper, formerly Speaker of the House, became President when President Rush and Vice President Carlson succumbed to the Bug within two months of each other. Before dying of natural causes many years later, Hopper signed an executive order making the Presidency a hereditary office until the State of Emergency ended and elections could be resumed. So George was America's first hereditary President, and his son John would likely be the second.

Back at work ten weeks later, Brad was assigned to light desk duty while he regained his strength. He spent much of his idle time thinking about Carla.

The obsession eventually drove him to perform, at considerable personal risk, an unauthorized database search that yielded her address and other personal information.

After returning to patrol duty, Brad would drive past Carla's apartment building every chance he got in the hope he would encounter her on her way to or from work and they would exchange a few words. His attraction to her continued unabated despite an upcoming repro assignment with Jane F-1891, which he was dreading.

Late one afternoon as he approached her building, he saw someone emerge and quickly head downtown. Based on body size and the color of the jumpsuit, he was certain it was Carla. Curious about her destination, he dismounted from his scooter and followed her on foot, rolling the scooter close to the buildings on the same side of the street she was on. There was no one else in sight.

Ten blocks down she went in the front door of a public library, which should have been locked. Brad removed his tranquilizer rifle from its scabbard and followed. As he opened the door he heard a faint buzz indicating the presence of an alarm system. He flipped off the rifle's safety switch and followed the sound of footsteps coming from a stairwell to his left. The footsteps stopped and a door slammed overhead just as he reached the stairs, but he could not tell what floor the sound came from. He searched the second floor and found nothing, but on the third he saw light coming from under a door midway down the corridor. He approached slowly, rifle at the ready, and opened the door.

The room was brightly lit and contained a large conference table surrounded by a dozen helmetless people looking in his direction. They were covering the lower halves of their faces with sheets of paper or scarves worn bandit style, and were seated around the table, except for a man standing in a corner pointing a sawed-off shotgun at him.

At the head of the table sat an elderly woman who had her white hair cut pageboy style and was wearing glasses with thick blue rims.

"Come on in, officer," she said with a gravelly voice. "Don't worry about the shotgun. We don't intend to hurt you. We just don't want you to arrest us."

"Who are you?"

"I'm the Librarian."

This made no sense. All the libraries had been shut down and there were no librarians.

"Suppose you tell me what's going on?" he said.

"Certainly. This is a meeting of the Heritage Preservation Book Club. You've not heard of us? Well, we're a national organization that has been teaching the humanities—literature, philosophy, the fine arts—to our members for almost three generations. The Federal Department of Education does a fine job with mathematics and science but it is understandably unwilling to expose the populace to anything that might make them unhappy with the status quo. So we try to keep the lamp of knowledge burning against the day when normalcy returns. We're always looking for new members. Perhaps you'd like to join."

"You need a special authorization to be here. I assume you don't have one."

"As a matter of fact we do. It's called the First Amendment to the United States Constitution."

"That was suspended by the State of Emergency."

"But the emergency is over. The A Bug was gone before you were born."

"That's ridiculous."

"Well, here my colleagues and I sit bare headed in close proximity to one another in a building without filtered air or air showers."

"Maybe you're suicidal."

"What about the President, his cabinet, and the other officials in Washington? None of them wear survival suits when they're not on television, and all of them live with their families and eat meat, poultry, and fresh vegetables."

"I don't believe you."

"We can show you pictures."

"They could be doctored."

"We could get you inside the Beltway, and you could see for yourself."

"You could avoid the Eye?"

"We could take care of that, yes, but, on second thought, I'm wondering whether it would be worth the trouble in your case. Maybe you're too indoctrinated to do your own thinking."

Brad bridled at the put-down. "Look, Miss whatever-your-name-is, the Government protects us and provides us with food, shelter, jobs, and medical care. There is little crime and life expectancies keep rising. Everyone, except you people, is content. What more is there for me to know? And anyway why would the Government lie to us about the Bug?"

"They started out with justification and good intentions. But once they had total control of us, it was hard to let go. Among themselves, I expect they rationalize the deception as being necessary to maintain the control and regimentation they need to grow the population up to some optimal level."

"There you go. What's wrong with that?"

"If you were to join us you would be able to answer your own question."

"Why would I ever want to become an anarchistic deviant? That's what you are, isn't it?"

"The President is calling us that, but we're not the dangerous revolutionaries he claims."

"But you have weapons. You wounded me and another Mountie."

"We have the one shotgun and, yes, we wounded you and your colleague because it was the only way to protect ourselves. Being transported to the farms is the equivalent of a death sentence to us."

"What about stealing RTEs?"

"As you may know, the Blue RTEs are adulterated with Nilid and other emotion-controlling drugs. So we steal yellows and greens and substitute them for the blues as often as we can."

She paused to allow Brad to process the information.

"Any other questions? No? Well then, I'm afraid we're going to have to tie you up now so you won't follow us when we leave."

Brad's response was to shoulder his rifle and point it at her.

"This could be tricky," said one of the men. "Those tranquilizer darts cause paralysis for about twelve hours, and if any of us doesn't show up for work they'll send a Mountie to investigate.

"No need to tie him up," Carla said as she lowered the large envelope that was concealing the lower half of her face. "He'll take me home. He knows who I am anyway. I'm sure he followed me here. We were paired for repro a few months ago, and I opted out."

There was a collective gasp, and the Librarian waved Carla over. The two of them had a whispered conversation, and when it became animated they left the room. After five minutes, they returned and Carla, looking pale, said, "Brad, would you please take me home? It's that or they'll have to shoot you."

He nodded his assent and lowered his gun, and they walked together in silence through the library to the street. When they reached the scooter, Brad mounted, and Carla climbed on behind him. Distracted by the pressure of her body against his, he did not think to radio for backup.

———

Brad pulled to the curb in front of Carla's building.

"Please come up, Brad. We have important things to talk about."

He nodded sullenly and followed her up the stairs. She used the air shower first and went into the apartment. Brad stepped into the vacated stall and, when the shower and air vacuum were done, removed his helmet and went inside. He found Carla waiting for him in her living room wearing loose fitting shorts and a T-shirt. Being a size too large, they made her look frail and vulnerable, and filled Brad with equal measures of tenderness and desire.

But seduction was the last thing on Carla's mind. She had absentmindedly removed her jumpsuit when she left the air shower because anxiety was making her sweat.

"You followed me, right?" she asked accusingly.

"Yes."

"Why? What made you suspicious?"

"I think about you a lot. I know it's not healthy, and I don't like it. But I can't help it."

*My god, he loves me,* she thought, and her fear evaporated."The Librarian was trying to get you to join us back there," she said gently. "If you did that, we could meet whenever we wanted. We could read the same books and talk about them. You could come over and listen to me play the piano."

"Is it true what the Librarian said about non-violence?"

"Yes, it is! We want to help people, to educate them, not to harm them. But that's not to say there aren't some members who are, well, less non-violent than others. But they're a minority."

Brad wanted to believe her. "You'll be able to teach me how to dodge the Eye so we can spend time together?"

"No, not teach. There'd be a procedure performed on your transponder by a doctor and a technician. It would be done in your apartment. The Librarian would arrange it."

Brad groaned. "Shit! If you've tampered with your transponders you're all sitting ducks. It's only a matter of time before Homeland Security starts checking them."

"They won't be able to tell. Trust me. We know what we're doing."

"You can't out-tech the Government. One way or another they'll eventually identify and capture all of you. Destroying you has become a priority, part of the war against extinction."

"That won't happen, Brad. It was only by accident you found us, and we'll be more careful now. If we stay out of the news, they'll forget about us."

He mournfully shook his head in disagreement. "No, they'll find you through your jerry-rigged transponders. It'll be easy for them." He saw he was frightening her.

"But don't worry, Carla. Whatever happens, I'll protect you. You're going to be okay."

"But you're thinking of reporting the others, right? You only saw part of their faces, but you're trained to remember details. You'll be able to identify some of them just from their eyes and hair, and they'll be arrested and questioned and forced to tell everything they know. Then all of us will be arrested and sent to the farms for the rest of our lives. Please don't make that happen, Brad. Join us, please." There were tears in her eyes.

He looked away. He was confused and wanted to be alone so he could sort things out. "I have to get back to the station or they'll come looking for me. They're probably trying to reach me on the scooter's radio." He picked up his helmet.

"But we haven't finished. You can call and make up an excuse. Get a little more time. Please, Brad." She was crying now.

"No, I can't. But don't worry. I'll think about everything you said before I do anything. I really will. But now I have to go."

Tears streamed down Carla's face as she watched him leave.

When the door closed she moaned, "Oh God," and began to sob. She walked across the apartment to its only window and looked down at a man standing in a doorway across the street holding a shopping bag, which she knew contained a sawed-off shotgun. Seeing her, he extended a hand with palm up inquiringly, and she responded by closing the blinds. She stood frozen in place for a few moments then gasped, "I can't do this to him," and jerked the blinds open, but the man was gone. She dashed across the apartment , through the shower, and out the door with no thought of donning her survival suit.

Meanwhile Brad was wrestling with his dilemma as he descended the three flights of stairs.

*I saw enough of the Librarian's face to make identifying her easy, and it's my duty to do that. Then she'll be taken into custody and forced to name the other club members, and Carla will be arrested and sent to the farms. Okay, but say I tell them that Carla's an informer and that she led me to the group after being inspired by the President's speech. They'd go easy on her. Punish her lightly, if at all, for joining in the first place. And, if we both asked for it, they might pair us for repro duty again as a reward. We could end up being partners for life. No, I'm dreaming. She won't lie to save her own neck and will never forgive me for turning them in. I just have to let her go. My repro with Jane F-1891 will help me forget. No, that's not going to happen. Carla's the only woman for me.*

As he reached the bottom of the stairs, Carla burst out onto the third floor landing and shouted his name.

"I'm coming back up, Carla," he answered. "I'll do what you want."

He heard the door to the street open behind him, and turned to face it.

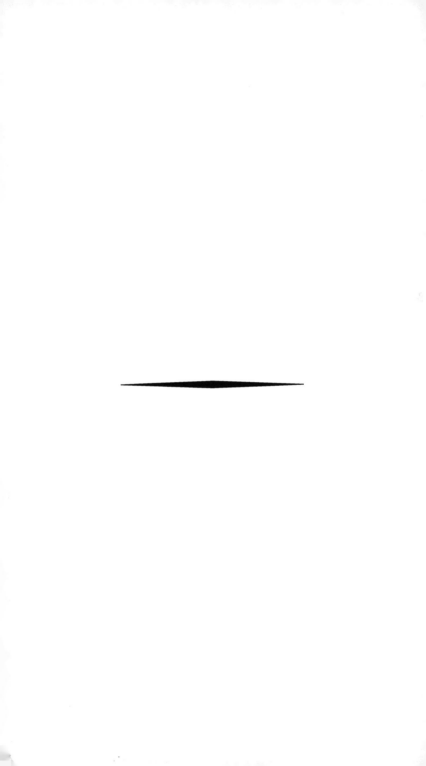

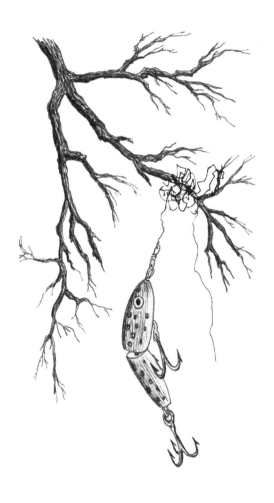

"I snagged his favorite bass lure in a
tree by the lake where it still hung."

# GRANDPA'S FINAL JOURNEY

The most indelible memory of my childhood is of the May morning following my grandfather's funeral. I, along with my parents, uncles, aunts, and cousins, had spent the previous night at my grandparents' lakeside house in Maine where we all had enjoyed many holidays and vacations together. I awoke that day to the loudest and most amazingly varied birdsong I had ever heard. I remember thinking that if Grandpa were there he could have told me which bird was singing which song.

On the previous day, neighbors and friends had come back to the house for lunch following Grandpa's funeral. When they left, Grandma, who didn't seem a bit sad, took one look at our long faces and said the best way to show our love for Grandpa would be to play games and carry on happily as we always did when at their house. She said if we did that he'd be looking down from heaven smiling, and we followed her advice.

Our high spirits carried over to the next morning, and so, while waiting for the sounding of the gong calling us to breakfast, we kids played badminton and tetherball, and our parents lounged in the Adirondack chairs by the lake.

Grandma had insisted on preparing breakfast on her own and, figuring it was good for her to keep busy, her daughters went along with this, even though they were afraid she'd make a mess of things. You see, for quite a while Grandma had been having what we all called "silly spells," which were probably early signs of the dementia that swallowed her up whole a few years later.

But her daughters needn't have worried. When we answered the gong, we found a delicious breakfast waiting for us on the large patio table overlooking the lake: fresh-squeezed orange juice, Grandma's famous granola-banana pancakes, butter, real maple syrup, bacon, coffee, tea, and milk. We could tell Grandma considered it a special occasion. She had set the table with a fine Irish linen tablecloth, freshly cut flowers, and her best glassware, china, and silverware. I heard my mother tell my Dad, "She was able to focus because this meant so much to her."

After devouring every last morsel, we all sat around the table and talked for a couple of hours about the good times spent with Grandpa. Everyone had stories to tell, and I remember them all. Mine was a funny one about how he groaned and then hugged me and said it was "okay" when I snagged his favorite bass lure in a tree by the lake where it still hung. Four-year-old Tori's remembrance was the most touching. She brought tears to our eyes when she said simply that she liked it when Grandpa pushed her on the swing, which we all had seen him do many times.

Then there was a lively discussion, which was fascinating to us kids, about what to do with Grandpa's ashes. All the men were opposed to just leaving them in the urn and favored scattering them at some beautiful place. A lot of possibilities were discussed, including a mountaintop in the Rockies, the Grand Canyon, and the Maine seacoast.

"But of course it's entirely your decision, Ma," my Uncle Bob eventually said. "So what do you think?"

"Well, those are all certainly very lovely places," Grandma said kindly. "But, you see, Dad and I never traveled much, and he was always happiest right here when his children and grandchildren came to visit. I know in my heart that the place he would most want to be is with all of you, so I have already taken care of his ashes and done it in the best possible way."

She smiled sheepishly and her gaze moved to the empty platter that had held the granola-banana pancakes. There was dead silence for about three seconds as everyone recalled the unusual graininess of the granola. Then all hell broke loose.

THE END

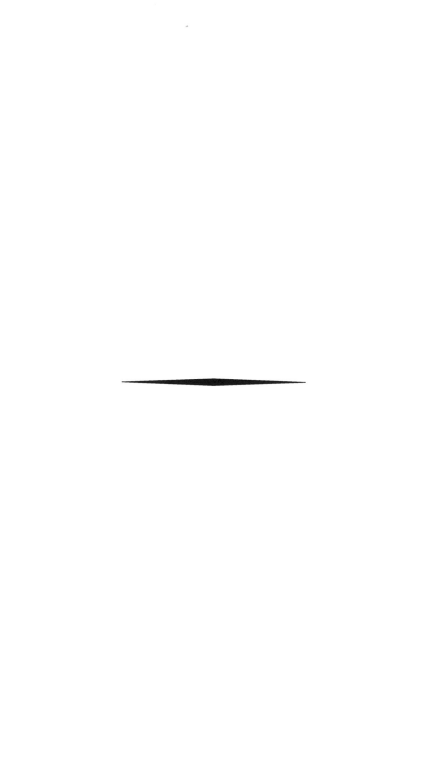

# ABOUT THE AUTHOR

Bill Finnegan earned BA and JD degrees from St. John's University in New York before embarking on a career that saw him serve as legal counsel for several major corporations, including USLIFE Holding Corp., American Broadcasting Companies, ITT World Communications, and AT&T.

After retiring he worked as a *pro bono* lawyer at Essex-Newark Legal Services representing the economically disadvantaged in Family Court litigation. In 2000 he was awarded an Equal Justice Medal by Legal Services of New Jersey for this work.

His novel, *Saving Frank Casey—A Semi-Comic Novel of Love, Religion, Politics, and Corporate Life*, was published in 2008. It was inspired by his experiences in the corporate world, with Legal

Services, and as a volunteer campaign worker for a presidential candidate in 2004.

Subsequently, he wrote eleven short stories that were published individually in *Chrysalis Reader*, *Studio* (Australia), *Barbaric Yawp*, *First Class*, *Cover of Darkness*, *Nocturnal Lyric*, *Shelter of Daylight*, *The Ultimate Writer*, *Concertina World* (England), *Tough Lit*, and *Adventures for the Average Woman*. Most of the stories appeared in more than one of the above publications. Two were nominated for the Pushcart Prize.

Bill and Terry, his wife of 55 years, have three children and six grandchildren and currently reside in Hamilton, New Jersey.

# ABOUT THE ARTIST

*Self-Portrait*

Creating fine art and doing graphic design have been Raven OKeefe's lifelong passions, as well as her profession, for over 30 years. She has been an artist since she was old enough to pick up a crayon to create unappreciated murals on her parents' walls.

Her works include both commercial art (e.g., book covers and illustrations) and fine art, which she does primarily in pen & ink with watercolor. Channeling her interest in and connection with Native American culture, she particularly enjoys using her artistry to capture the intrinsic spirit, as well as the appearance, of both wildlife and domesticated animals. Her pet portraits are in continual demand, and she is at work on a book of drawings and discussion of totem animals.

Raven and her husband operate Wolston Farm in Scio, Oregon, where they raise sheep, keep a flock of surly chickens, and raise and train Border Collies to help them manage their flock and to run in competitions.

32845809R00090

Made in the USA
Lexington, KY
04 June 2014